DEATH AT THE DOG SHOW
DOG DETECTIVE - A BULLDOG ON THE CASE MYSTERY

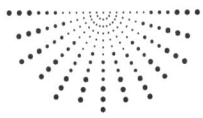

ROSIE SAMS

SWEETBOOKHUB.COM

DOG DETECTIVE - A BULLDOG ON THE CASE

So many of my readers enjoyed meeting Lola Ramsay and Sassy, the Lilac Frenchie, that I knew I had to write more books with these wonderful characters.

You can now grab the first 6 Bulldog on the Case books in one great value box set and also FREE with Kindle Unlimited

Sassy is modeled on Lila, my Lilac French Bulldog. Lila had been returned to her breeder as she was unwanted. At the time, I was looking for an older, small, short-haired dog to rescue. Something I could cuddle, that would keep me company while I was writing. When I met Lila I fell in love with her and that as they say, was that.

Can you believe that anyone would not want her? She is the sweetest little bundle of love you could ever meet. Well, someone's loss was my gain.

Lila is a joy to live with, though she does like to pinch my socks. Nothing makes her happier than getting out of bed and stealing my socks. It has become such a joke that I put a pair on the bed just for this.

Now, all I needed was a new name and so I asked you, my wonderful readers, to come up with a name. There were some great ideas but the one that suited the character the most was Sassy Pants by Sandra H. Thank you, Sandra, we love the name.

I'm so pleased that my wonderful cover designer has managed to bring photos of Lila/Sassy to life for the covers. Much of what Sassy does comes from Lila; you will have to decide if I can hear her talking. I hate to admit it, but I talk to her constantly.

Read on for my next book, where Sassy and Lola are staying in a sleepy British village with a friend. I hope you enjoy it.

Join my newsletter to grab some free short stories.

COME TO WOOF

Come to Woofs"You must come to Woofs," Una Freeman said as she sipped her tea. The dog show judge was perched on the edge of the sofa in Alice's conservatory. With a big smile on her face, she flicked her long, black fringe off her huge round black glasses. Her pencil-thin eyebrows were raised in question.

Alice clapped her hands together. "That would be wonderful, we should all go. It would make a marvelous day out, what do you think, Tilly, Lola, and of course, little Sassy? Maybe we could even enter Sassy into something?"

"I would be bestest," Sassy said, sitting and staring up at Alice with her tongue sticking out. The little Lilac

Frenchie turned to look at Lola who gave her a smile of encouragement.

Alice was the absolute opposite of Una. The judge's black hair was around 5 inches long and styled both beautifully and fashionably around her face. She wore a smart black skirt suit and neat court shoes. Though she was good company, Una was reserved and dignified. Alice was a different kettle of fish; she had short, curly blonde hair and was wearing a purple shell suit with an orange V across the front and bright orange trainers. Her blond hair was a mess of tight curls cradled around her head. Her personality was as bright as her clothing and there was always a smile on her face.

"Oh, I'm so sorry but there is an intensive qualification to compete at Woof's." Una patted her leg and Sassy trotted over. Una reached down and stroked the little Frenchie. "I still think you should come. You will enjoy it, and I can show you around after I've judged the Best in Show competition."

The little French bulldog rolled over onto her back making the most gorgeous grunty, groany noises to say that she appreciated the fuss.

"I think that would be a great idea," Tilly said. She was the oldest of the group, with short, neat grey hair, today she was wearing a brown tweed skirt and a white blouse. She peered through her round glasses at Lola, pushing the glasses back up her short nose, which she wrinkled as she waited for a reply.

"It sounds like fun, would Sassy be able to come?" Lola was the youngest of the group, and though she had seen a lot of the world, she often felt inexperienced around her friends. They knew so much about the world they lived in. Lola ran a hand down her own hair. It was long and black and straight but it still seemed to have a life of its own and today there seemed to be a lot of static in the air. Tendrils of her hair were floating away from her head and it was distracting.

"I believe she's your service dog?" Una asked.

"Yes, she is." Lola ran her hands over her jeans.

"She's so clever," Alice said. "So many people misjudge her, with her big eyes, funny face, and stubby little body, but that little dog has got a good head on her shoulders. She has helped us out on many an occasion. She has to come."

"Not stubby, strong." Sassy sat on her butt and stuck her back legs out along with her tongue. It was her protest sit and Lola couldn't help but smile.

Una chuckled. "Of course, she can come; as a service dog, she is allowed in almost anywhere. It would be great to have you all there and nice to have some support after judging the Best in Show."

"I get the feeling there's a story there?" Tilly asked. "Is support really needed?"

"No, not really. You judge the dogs on their merits, the dog you see before you. Not all do, sometimes friends give friends prizes. However, I don't agree with that. I am a big believer that we are there to improve the health of dogs and that does upset some people. There are those that breed for looks alone and we should still be breeding for function."

"Oh, I totally agree," Alice said. "I have seen some things but it is better now and Best in Show must just have fabulous dogs in the competition."

"Oh, it does, which makes the choice harder." Una grinned a little. "The problem is, that everybody loves their own dog. Everybody thinks their dog is the best. Some of these people are very serious. I have had threats in the past."

"Threats, my goodness, how awful." Alice's hand was at her heart.

"Oh, don't worry, they are a nice bunch really. Just at times, tempers get the better of them. Mark Duncan, now, he is a man with a temper. Luckily, for him, his little poodle is a star. Things would have to go very badly for it not to win."

"Do you really get threats?" Alice was looking worried.

"Everyone expects to win, I guess that is what top-class competitors are like. If they didn't believe that they would win, they would never be good enough to put the hours in to get there in the first place. Don't look so worried, Alice, I can cope with it." Una smiled. "Being a judge is usually straightforward and most competitors take the judge's decision as final."

"Most!" Tilly did not look convinced.

"I bitesy them, if they bad," Lola heard in her mind and looked down to see Sassy bearing her teeth as she growled. She was, however, now lying on her back so her jowls were flopping open showing her tiny white teeth, so she looked anything but scary.

Lola chuckled. "I think Sassy will protect you."

Una's eyes opened wide and so did her mouth as she looked down at the growling Frenchie with her legs waving in the air. "I feel safer already." She chuckled.

"So, do you get threats often?" Lola asked.

"No, of course not. I was silly to even mention it and this country is so much better than others. I might be judging in Mexico and then in Qatar soon. Now, they are very serious, and sometimes it can get a little worrying. Sometimes they ask things of you that you would rather not do."

Lola was intrigued and wanted to ask if she meant illegal things, or perhaps just cheating? Before she could, Alice was talking and she decided such a conversation would spoil the moment.

"My goodness, why would you travel to such places?" Alice asked. "I prefer to stay here in Great Britain, I know what I'm getting here.

"It will be fine, I love judging dogs and, though I hate to say it, such appointments are very lucrative. It is for my retirement."

"I thought you were already retired," Tilly said.

A look of sadness crossed Una's face. "I was; unfortunately, my pension fund... well, I trusted the wrong person and it has gone."

"Oh, that is awful, maybe Lola could investigate it for you," Alice said pointing at Lola.

"That is very kind but there is no point. The people were from some foreign country and I'm told there is no way I could ever get it back. I was a fool, taken for a ride... I just thought I knew better. I'm sure you've heard it all before. I thought it couldn't happen to me, that I was clever and on the ball... but they were very good, very professional, and then... well, then it was all gone!" A wistful look crossed her face and she bit her bottom lip.

"Unfortunately, I doubt I could help, anyway, Lola said. "It's not something I know much about. I'm so sorry to hear this."

"No problem!" Una put a smile back on her face. It looked like it took some effort. "So, there it is, if I wish to keep my house, I have to judge at a few shows for the next few years. The one in Qatar will give my savings a good boost and with the Mexico one, I'm told that they want to discuss a business deal with me. Something that could be very lucrative. I have a few online meetings and calls and I should be seeing representatives from both countries at Woofs. They want to talk to me, I'm hopeful that it is judging or training judges that they are after, and that it will be enough to secure my future."

"That sounds wonderful," Alice said. "If there's anything we can do, you must ask."

"I will, of course, I will."

Lola picked up on the word "hoping" and wondered what else Una might be asked to do. It was worrying, Una was obviously stressed about it, but she was hiding it well.

Lola looked down to see Sassy rubbing against her leg. There was a look of worry in the Frenchie's amber eyes.

"Lady worried, not telling all," Sassy said in Lola's mind.

Lola tended to agree. She looked over at Una and there was definitely tension in her eyes. It could easily be a touch of shame and worry over losing her savings, but, could something more sinister be going on?

SPIDEY SENSE

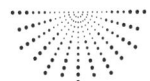

3 **weeks later.**

Lola could tell that Sassy was excited to be making her way into the crowded exhibition hall. The parking lot, or car park as she must start to call it, was huge. So huge that they had taken a bus to get to the hall and were now queuing along with many other people.

"It looks like it's going to be a lovely day," Alice said, brushing a floating seed away from the front of her shell suit. Today's was lavender with a pink stripe across the middle and she had matching fluorescent pink trainers.

Tilly was wearing a smart steel gray outfit that fit her perfectly and was a contrast to Alice's color.

"I do like your pants," Lola said.

Tilly's eyes opened a little beneath her round glasses. They seemed to fill the lenses and then she brushed at her butt. "I didn't realize they were showing, is it VPL?"

Lola could see that her friend was quite upset and wondered what she had done wrong. Sassy was lying on the ground covering her eyes with her paws. "You stepped in it," Sassy said.

Lola wanted to ask the Frenchie what she had said wrong because the last thing she wanted to do was distress Tilly.

It was Alice who let out a roar of laughter. "Oh, you mean trousers!"

"You do?" Tilly asked, looking altogether relieved.

"Of course, what did you think I meant?" Now Lola's cheeks were burning.

"In Britain, pants are underwear..." Alice chuckled again and shook her head as if she was humoring a child. Luckily, Lola knew that she meant no offense. "We don't mention people's pants in polite conversation."

"I'm sorry." Lola shrugged and looked at Tilly.

Her eyes were back to their normal size. Tilly pushed her glasses back up her nose and smiled. It scrunched up her face and Lola was praying that Sassy would not say Moley; if she did, Lola knew that she would start to giggle and that just wouldn't suit the mood. With that, as if on cue, she heard her phone tinkle with a new notification. Though she knew she had to answer them, something was holding her back.

The queue had moved on and the people behind them were crowding them to herd the three ladies and a Frenchie forward.

Alice laughed. "And whatever you do, don't call a bum bag a fanny pack. I nearly punched the guy at the airport."

"I don't understand," Lola said. "Why?"

Alice was glowing, her cheeks brighter than the stripe across her shell suit. "A bum is a butt, or a rear or a bottom, a fanny is a lady's private parts."

"Oh!" Lola chuckled.

"When I arrived in Denver, this big strapping man asked to look in my fanny pack." Alice was giggling so much she couldn't continue and the three of them stepped forward once more hooting with laughter.

"I hope it's cool inside?" Tilly said, "and I'm already fancying a cup of tea. Who's with me?"

"Will there be cake?" Sassy woofed at their feet.

"I guess you would like some." Tilly chuckled and leaned down and stroked her head.

"You hear me?" Sassy asked but they were moving forward and Tilly was no longer looking at her. Sassy's bottom lip stuck out and she plonked her bottom down on the tarmac. "Not hear me!"

Lola reached down and picked her up. "Sorry, other people can't hear you but I can and you know how much I love you."

"Lovey luv you too," Sassy whispered into her ear.

"Good. Let's go inside and we will see what we can find," she whispered into Sassy's ear hoping her friends would not hear the conversation.

The Frenchie snuggled against her cheek and gave her a kiss. "Lovey love you."

"Exhibitors are to use the other entrance," a tall man in a suit said to Lola and then his eyes widened when he took another look at Sassy. "Oh, I apologize, I didn't realize." With this, he turned and was gone.

"What was all that about?" Tilly asked.

Lola was unsure too but she knew that Alice, their fountain of knowledge, would probably know.

"I don't want to say, I don't want to upset Sassy." Alice shrugged.

"You won't," Lola said for now she was really curious.

"It is because Sassy, is… well, she is not a recognized color," Alice said.

"I don't understand." Lola was really confused now. Though she thought Sassy was beautiful, she had never really thought about her color, it just was. So how could it not be recognized?

"The official colors recognized by the Kennel Club for French Bulldogs are brindle, fawn, or pied. Sassy has what they call mutant genes."

"Me not turtle," Sassy said.

Lola almost laughed, for the way Sassy had wrinkled up her face in disgust, she actually looked a little like a turtle. "That sounds worrying." Lola wondered if this could be a problem for her little pal, not that she could do anything about it.

"No, not really. These exotic, as they call them, colored dogs can be more prone to skin problems but little Sassy is as healthy as a horse. The more... exotic colors have what are called diluted genes. These change the colors from one to the other. Una told me all about it but it is quite complicated and don't worry, Sassy is fine."

Lola breathed a sigh of relief. The last thing she wanted to think about was her little friend being ill. Luckily, Sassy was the picture of health. Even though she was always looking for treats she ran like the wind and was slim and full of muscle. She was always chasing a bird or a squirrel and was surprisingly fast. As well as having amazing endurance. Lola knew that the little dog would keep going longer than she would.

Before too long, they had made their way into the exhibition center. The entrance was a large area milling with people. The noise was a buzz of conversation and for a moment, Lola closed her eyes to drown it out. Tilly was looking up and Lola followed her eyes. Signs indicated the different halls; they were looking for hall 1.

"Ah, there is Una," Alice said pointing across the crowd of people.

Lola looked down, Sassy did not seem phased by the noise and number of people, she was sitting and looking around. "Cake, that way," she said and indicated with her eyes when she noticed Lola looking at her.

"Soon," Lola whispered and they crossed the throng, in the opposite direction, to join Una. Sassy was only a little reluctant to move away from the cake stall.

Una was wearing a very smart herringbone skirt suit in black and white with neat court shoes. Her hair was styled to perfection. Though she must be in her 60s the fashionable style had her black hair flicking out from her face. "Morning," she called. "I will just show you to the ring, I got you special seats with a great view. You will be very close. Then I will have to run. Judging doesn't start for an hour but there is much to do."

Una's hand went to her stomach and Lola could have sworn she grimaced but she turned away so quickly that she couldn't be sure.

"Here." Una turned back and handed them each a ticket that was in the Woofs special blue.

They followed her through the crowd, sometimes being bumped and pushed but Tilly and Alice seemed to handle it well. Sassy was fine too, darting around feet that came too close and then seeing a gap and trotting along proudly in front of them. That seemed to clear the way a little.

They went up some stairs, and out into another arena. The sides of this hall were filled with benches. Alice had told Lola about these. They were the areas for the dogs to rest between judging. There was a bench on the ground that was partitioned off for each dog. The show dogs were relaxed and comfortable on the benches being very used to them. Each lot of benches was for a specific breed; there were huskies, terriers, Samoyeds, greyhounds, and others. Then there was the bench for the Best in Show qualifying dogs.

As they walked, Lola couldn't help but watch Una. The woman's movements were stiff and she seemed to be clutching at her stomach, even though she was clearly trying to hide it. There was a slight sheen of sweat on her neck; what was wrong?

They carried on through the hall, the way much easier with a Frenchie escort.

"Are you excited?" Alice asked Una.

"Of course." Una smiled briefly and then carried on walking, she was in a hurry.

"Who's going to win?" Alice's face was eager with excitement.

"You know I can't discuss that." Una smiled and then grimaced and they continued to weave their way through the crowds.

Sassy scratched at Lola's leg.

"She worried," Sassy said. "Bad worried, scaredy cat!"

Lola tried not to chuckle at the Frenchie's colorful language. She had noticed that Una was not quite her normal self. Her voice was a little higher, her words a little clipped, she was holding her stomach, and she had glanced around a few times. The logical explanation was that it was nerves. This judging appointment was probably one of the most prestigious, if not in the world, then in the United Kingdom.

Una looked fine now. She walked through the crowd as if she owned the place, her head high as people tried to get her attention. Only occasionally did she stop to stare at someone. It was hard to tell if she was looking for something or just a little hyped, because of the magnitude of the event.

One of the poodle handlers, a heavy-set bald man in a pink suit, almost stepped in front of her as he was fluffing his honey-colored dog's puffy fur to perfection.

Una neatly side-stepped and totally ignored him.

Lola noticed that Sassy had stopped, her eyes wide as she took in the dog's elaborate coat. "Don't stare," she whispered.

Sassy backed away before quickly running past the sumptuous-looking poodle.

As they walked, Lola noticed a prickling on the back of her neck. It was a feeling she had been used to when she was in the military. It usually meant danger, or that she was being watched. Turning but trying not to be too obvious, she checked the hall. Over to the left two men were staring. They were dark-haired with mustaches and olive skin. They wore dark suits and seemed stiff, and out of place. Their eyes had the seasoned glance of one who had seen action. Though one of them seemed nervous as a party bumped into him. They were not used to crowded places. Were these the Mexicans that Una had mentioned? Were they waiting to see her? Was this what she was worried about?

Lola continued her scanning of the crowd, a few of the competitors were also watching Una. She guessed this was understandable. Maybe they were assessing her mood for the competition ahead. Would the judge's mood alter how you showed your dog? Lola had to admit that she knew very little about this.

Across the other side of the hall, was a delegation that looked like they could be from Qatar. They were wearing the traditional ankle-length throbe in a variety of pastel colors, light blue, cream, fawn, and two white. The robes looked expensive, and their heads were covered with chequered keffiyehs in black or red. There were five of them altogether and two were watching Una, tracking her as she made her way through the hall. They also looked like muscle to Lola, men that had seen action and could handle themselves, but was her imagination just running away with her? Was she seeing trouble for the sake of it?

Then her mind went back to Una saying she had received threats. Could either of these groups be the people that were making threats? Did Lola need to keep her eyes on them? Before she could give it much more thought they had made their way to the entrance of the main display ring. This was where the dogs would be shown in about an hour.

Una talked to a suited official and explained that they were her guests. The man almost bowed and opened the gate allowing them to pass. His eyebrows rose as he saw Sassy, but he didn't pass comment.

Una showed them up the stairs and passed many rows of seats to some seats that were halfway up in the center of the arena. "These are the best seats. There is a walkway between you so you will easily see over the crowd." She smiled at Tilly and Alice who, though not short, were not that tall. "I have to go now; I suggest you go and have a look around and get back here around 11 am. Have a wonderful day. I will see you after the judging. I will have to do some interviews but it should be around 1. Wait here, I will come to you."

"Fabulous," Alice said. "Good luck," she called as Una turned to walk away once more grasping her stomach.

Lola let her take a step and then followed her. "Una."

The judge turned and smiled. "I don't have long, but can I help?"

"Forgive me, if I'm talking out of turn, but are you worried about something?" Lola asked.

Something flashed across Una's eyes but she hid it before Lola could work out what it was.

"I'm fine, don't worry, maybe a little nervous."

"If you are in any trouble, talk to me, I can help."

Una stared at Lola for a few moments and indecision flashed in her brown eyes. Then she flicked her hair and shook her head. "It's not worry. It was, but I'm fine... just a stomach ache, probably nerves," Una said. Seeing that Lola was not convinced she continued, "Don't worry about it, all will be fine."

Before Lola could say anymore Una turned to walk away.

As the judge made her way down the steps Lola couldn't help but feel worried. Something had set off her spidey senses and she couldn't shake the feeling that something was wrong.

"Who's for tea and cake?" Alice asked.

"Me, me, me, me, me," Sassy woofed as she span in circles on the narrow walkway. Taking one spin too close to the edge, she tumbled over jumping up and looking a little shocked. "Meant to do that," she said as they all started laughing.

DONUTS

"What do you all fancy for a snack?" Alice asked as they made their way to the edges of the hall. It was surrounded by eating outlets and the smells were amazing.

"Do I smell donuts?" Lola asked.

"Yes, they do smell good," Tilly said. "I love them, warm, sugary, melt in the mouth. Who's up for donuts?"

"Me, me, me." Sassy was jumping up and down in front of them.

"I think that's settled." Alice was smiling at the Frenchie.

They traced their way to the donut stall by the scent. Lola was amazed at the myriad of amazing stalls that were in the hall. Apart from the eateries, there was everything for dogs, from food, collars, leads, herbal supplements, pajamas, and the toys.

Sassy's eyes were popping out of her head as she spotted a huge 2-foot-tall purple octopus. The octopuses were her favorite toy, she had three little ones at home, all in various states of de-fluffing. One was simply a furry husk. But these were huge and her eyes were almost as big!

The toys were fabulous as each leg had a squeaker and some plastic inside that made them rustle when chewed. The body was soft and fluffy and lovely to pull all of the stuffing out of!

"Oh, wow!" Sassy was staring up at the magnificent-looking toy. "Can I?"

Lola couldn't resist. "I have got to get one of these for Sassy."

"It is four times as big as her." Alice raised an eyebrow.

"She would love it," Tilly said, "But let's eat first, and grab it on our way to watch the competition. It will save having to carry it."

Sassy pawed at Tilly's leg. "I carry toy, I keep it." Her eyes were wide and pleading.

"Later," Lola said and scooped Sassy into her arms. She could feel that the little bulldog was stiff and sad. "Donuts, first," she whispered into her ear.

Sassy licked her face. "You bribe me, still want leggy thing."

Lola cuddled her close as they made their way through the hall.

"Oh, look at these." Alice said as they queued for the donuts.

The stall next to them was loaded with action cameras that could be strapped to a dog's harness, amongst other things. The video quality was amazing. They were showing films of various doggy adventures. On some of the videos, you could just see the outline of the dog's ears. It was delightful to get the dog's eye view.

"Phew!" Lola said. They had a hefty price tag, and even though she still had hardly touched her trust fund and the money she received from a Russian gangster, she didn't like to spend for nothing.

"They would be great for your work," Alice said. "You could train Sassy to go investigate for you."

Lola chuckled and had another look at the cameras, maybe they could come in useful, but not today.

With the drinks and the donuts, they found an area to sit and took seats at a nearby table.

"These are delicious," Alice said.

Lola's phone let out another notification that she had received a text. She had a quick look and tried not to sigh. It was from Linc. A man she had met a few weeks ago and who had been messaging her ever since. At first, she had answered back but so far she hadn't agreed to meet him. She wasn't sure why! Well, apart from the fact that men either betrayed her or died.

"Just as I remember them from years ago." Tilly was licking her lips. "Are you going to answer that?"

"Not tried yet!" Sassy's voice was sad and heartbreaking. Lola pulled off a little bit, blew on it to make sure it was not too warm, and passed it down to her pal. The little Frenchie had distracted her and she hoped she could get away with not answering Tilly. However, her friend was sharp, and she would not get away with it forever.

Sassy chomped away on the morsel, little nom nom noises along with grunts and groans of pure pleasure were coming from her.

"She certainly enjoys her food," Alice said. "We should all be more like dogs."

Lola chuckled. "We could learn a lot from them. They know how to live in the moment."

"She delights in everything, I want to try to be like her," Alice said.

Tilly choked a little, spluttering as she put down her coffee.

"What?!" Alice asked.

"You are exactly like her, you live for the moment and enjoy everything." Tilly was shaking her head but there was a smile on her face.

Lola had to admit that Alice was special in this way. She was always happy, always excited and she delighted in everything she came across. Now that Tilly mentioned it, she could see a lot of the dog's character in Alice.

"I think that's the best compliment I've ever had." Alice was wearing a big smile.

Sassy made her way around the table, sitting in front of Tilly and letting out a little groan.

Lola could hear. "So hungry, feed me." To the rest of them, it was just a series of grumbles.

"You are so cute." Tilly passed down a little bit of donut and then broke off a half dozen pieces and put them to cool.

Sassy took the morsel and closed her eyes savoring the delicious treat. Across the table, Alice took a bite, and she too closed her eyes and had such an expression of pure pleasure on her face that it reminded Lola of the film When Harry Met Sally.

Sassy finished her morsel and went around the table to Alice. Pawing at her leg, when she wasn't instantly noticed. Alice chuckled and handed down a bit of donut.

"Has Una said anything else about any threats?" Lola asked.

Alice's eyes snapped up. Knowing that she had begged all the donut from her that she would, for now, Sassy came back to Lola.

"No, she only mentioned it that one time." Alice shook her head and there was concern on her face. "Do you think there's trouble?"

Sassy was pawing Lola's leg, she absently handed down a bit of donut and the Frenchie started her circuit once more. She had learned how to play them all, going from one to the other again and again.

"I'm sure it's nothing. I just thought she might be a little worried." Lola smiled to show that she was not really bothered. She didn't want to scare her friends, or spoil the day, but she couldn't shake the feeling that something was wrong.

"I'm sure it's just pre-competition nerves," Tilly said. "Either that or you are missing a murder." She chuckled and handed Sassy a bit of a donut. The Frenchie was on her third lap of the table.

"I'm sure you're right," Lola said and tried to push the uneasy feelings away. She had lost track of the two groups of men that had worried her. Now, thinking about it they were doing nothing wrong, they were probably just excited about the competition like everyone else was.

Sassy tapped at her leg. Lola looked down and smiled at her little friend. "You must be full."

"Not full, empty." Sassy smiled up at her.

"If you have any more donuts you will be too fat to move." Lola blew her cheeks out to make a fat face.

"You are so funny, the way you talk to that dog," Tilly said. "It is very charming.

"That little pup couldn't be fat if it tried. Look at her muscles," Alice said. "She never stops."

Sassy stepped back from the table and it was almost as if she was clenching her muscles and posing like a bodybuilder. Lola had to admit that she was a fit little dog.

"Oh, she is so funny," Alice said. "I swear she can understand us. Give her some more, she's fading away."

Sassy dropped onto the floor and lay still as if she were gone. When nothing happened she raised her head. Lola couldn't resist and Tilly chuckled at the Frenchie's antics.

Lola laughed and handed Sassy down a little bit of donut. As she did she could see the bald man who was titivating the poodle earlier; he was staring daggers into a corner. When she followed his eyes she saw Una talking to one of the officials. It looked like being a dog show judge did not make you well-liked.

But this meant nothing, Lola pushed her feelings of foreboding down and sipped at her coffee. Nothing was going to happen, this was just a dog show!

THE SHOW

It was almost an hour later and they were sitting in their seat looking down at the arena. The famous blue carpet was currently bare. There was an excited buzz in the air as people took their seats and at Lola's feet, Sassy was happily sucking on the foot of a huge purple octopus!

She liked to chomp her teeth and then suck on the toy and she would do it for hours — if you let her. She also liked to carry the toys around and throw them in the air, but that was not possible here amongst the seats.

"Do you need a drink?" Lola asked.

"No, busy," the words were squeezed out between sucks and Sassy didn't lift her jowls off the toy.

The occasional squeak was turning heads and Lola knew she would have to take the toy off her before the competition began. That could cause some disappointment.

The seats were filling up fast and there was a buzz amongst the crowd. Lola could hear people all around her, some were talking about their favorite, others just chatting in general or admiring the dogs but not sure who would win.

Alice came rushing along the row, causing people to stand as she squeezed herself in. "I bought these." She waved a paper packet.

Sassy raised her head, whatever was in the packet was to her liking.

"I thought they would keep our little munchkin quiet, during judging." Alice handed the packet over to Lola.

Lola opened the bag and there was a strong smell of beef. Inside, were some fudge-colored sticks. "What are they?"

"Air-dried pizzle," Alice said in a loud voice.

"What is that?" Lola asked.

"I wouldn't ask." Tilly raised her eyebrows. "Sassy will love them and they are great for cleaning her teeth.

"Oh, it's starting," Alice said as the lights went down.

The whole crowd hushed as darkness settled over the arena for a few moments before the ring in front of them was lit up with blue light. Around the showing area, were electronic boards, also in blue and white. A white dog trotted across the blue background along with the word Woofs.

"This is so exciting," Tilly said.

Lola handed a pizzle to Sassy. For a moment, she thought the Frenchie would not take it, she didn't want to let go of her new toy. However, she was drawn by the scent and took the treat delicately, curling down on the octopus to chew it.

"Sorry," Lola said and pulled the toy out from under her.

"Not fair!"

"You can have it back later."

"Ssshhh." Came from behind them.

Over the loudspeaker system, a compère came on and introduced Una. "We are so lucky to have the very experienced Una Freeman judging for us this year. She is escorted into the ring by the chairman of Woofs, John Blackmore."

Una and a tall man with gray hair, wearing a black suit came into the arena. They were lit up by a spotlight as they crossed the blue carpet. The crowd cheered for a few moments, it looked like Una was well-liked.

"Una is one of the most experienced judges in this country, and possibly, the most experienced in the world. She is well known for her expertise in all breeds, especially the utility group and she is famous for her Dalmatians. Una has bred Dalmatians for over 40 years and has done much to improve the health and recognition of the breed. She has judged here at Woofs twice before and we are delighted to welcome her back this year."

"Her friend is showing that awful Labrador," a woman's voice came from behind Lola.

"It doesn't have a chance," came a reply. "I can't even believe it qualified by winning the group."

"Ssshh," Alice said.

Lola leaned over and asked Alice what the group was.

"Ahh, there are 7 groups. Goldie, the Labrador in question, would have won the gundog group at this show on Wednesday."

"Thanks." Lola turned her mind back to the ring and was surprised that she felt a buzz of excitement, along with a touch of worry. Something still told her that trouble was ahead.

The compère was continuing to tell people about Woofs and the show and Una. The ring before them was dark, lit only with blue light and traced over with spotlights. The ceiling was filled with twinkling stars.

Lola was half listening and also watching the ring. In the shadow of darkness, boards, 7 in total, were being placed across the other side of the ring. Then a table was brought out holding a huge silver trophy.

Lola noticed that there were 4 dark-suited and very smart men standing one in the middle of each side of the arena. They reminded her of butlers and she wondered what their purpose was.

Glancing back she could see that Una was standing near the boards with the chairman and a different man with a clipboard.

"Scribing for Una is Mick Robertshaw," the compère was still talking. "Another veteran of Woofs. Mick has scribed in ten Best of Show competitions, more than any other scribe. He will listen to Una, and make notes on anything she says. That way, she can look back at it, nothing is missed or forgotten, and she can use the comments after the competition.

Big screens were placed strategically around the ring so that everyone could see the action. At the moment, the one in front of Lola had Una on it. She was chatting with the man next to her, Mick. Was she worried? Lola studied her, but she seemed ok. There was no flicking of her eyes, no peering into the crowd or searching for danger, no wringing of her hands or other nervous gestures. In fact, the two of them were talking and smiling. Maybe, Lola had just imagined a danger.

"Relax." Tilly touched her arm.

"Sorry."

A spotlight zoomed across to the entrance of the ring.

"Excitement is rising as the best of the best are about to come into the ring," the compère began. "There are 7 dog groups, made up from the 220 breeds who compete here at Woofs. The winner of each group has been chosen over the last few days. These most magnificent of dogs will now be judged against each other, to gain the coveted crown, Best in Show title.

"Oh, here we go." A hush settled over the arena as if everyone held their breath.

"First into the arena is the winner of the working group, the boxer known at home as Big Bruce."

"Oh, I didn't expect a boxer," Alice said. "Isn't he beautiful?"

The big and muscular red dog seemed to strut across the carpet, he was confident with his head high. As he strutted around the ring, his lead was held up high by an equally muscular and tall man with dark hair, a serious face, and a goatee. He was wearing a black trouser suit that seemed to sparkle beneath the spotlight. It was very nice and a little over the top for Lola's liking but she understood that this was a once-in-a-lifetime experience. His black shoes were either highly polished or also sparkly as they caught the light from time to time. It pulled the eye from the dog, but even so, the team looked spectacular.

"That's Peter Bower," Alice whispered. "I believe this is the first time he has won the group. Bruce is a playful dog but the rumor is, that Peter has a temper. I heard that he pushed another competitor once when he thought he should have won."

Lola took her eyes off the dog and let them fall on his handler. The man looked anything but threatening as he pranced around the ring with his dog. It was almost as if he was leaping from foot to foot, there was a big smile on his face and his emotions spoke of pride and joy. He pranced almost as much as the dog and was light on his feet for a such big man.

The boxer ran a full circuit of the ring, covering the ground quickly and effortlessly. The suited men, who were placed around it, guided him from one of them to the next. It seemed a little silly to Lola; surely, the competitors knew what they were doing. However, she guessed it was also rather quaint and at least she now knew why they were there. For a moment, earlier, she had thought they might be there for security. She really was letting her imagination get the better of her.

Once he had done his circuit, Peter took Bruce and stood before the furthest of the boards.

Una had been studying the dog intensely and had no time for anything else. As he stopped, the man put the dog into a stack. Alice had explained this to Lola earlier, it was the showing stance. The dog stood square with its head and tail high and its back legs stretched out a little.

It was a beautiful pose. Una was reviewing the animal and occasionally muttering to Mick who scribbled on his clipboard.

The spotlight left Bruce and traveled back to the entrance. Once more there was a buzz amongst the crowd as the spotlight was left empty for a few seconds.

"Next we have the Red Irish Terrier, the winner of the terrier group. Casey is a beautiful and feisty dog according to her handler, Paddy McKiernan. Casey means brave in battle and Paddy assures us that this little beauty would be the bravest of them all."

The people sitting behind them cheered as the little dog bounced into the ring. "Look at Casey go," one of the women said.

"So beautiful, she could win this and Paddy is looking great," her friend answered.

Lola was surprised at the comment.

"I think they have a good chance," Alice said.

"These two are one of the front runners with the crowd today," the compère said. "They traveled from Ireland, just three days ago, and it was no surprise when they won the terrier group. Casey looks like one brave little dog," the compère said as they made their way around the ring.

Lola had loved Bruce but she thought the little terrier was stunning. A beautiful red-brown coat, a high head, and tail carriage, and her legs just seemed to glide across the carpet. In contrast, Paddy was short and a little overweight. He didn't glide but seemed to almost hobble around the arena. Unlike the previous man, Paddy was wearing a very non-descript brown suit.

The team traveled across the famous blue carpet surprisingly quickly to stand next to the boxer, at board number 2.

Alice leaned over to talk to them both as Una took her time looking over the terrier.

"This is a super little dog, according to my friend." Alice winked as she didn't want to mention that her friend was the judge. "This dog has a real chance today. Paddy, however, is another one renowned for his temper," Alice whispered and flashed her eyes at the people behind them. "Though, it seems he has some fans."

"We should decide who we think will win," Tilly said. "Make a little wager out of it."

"Oh, that would be fun!" Alice answered.

"My pizzle is the winner, followed by big leggy toy," Sassy said, though the words were muffled as she had not stopped chewing.

Lola chuckled and nodded at her friends.

The spotlight arched back to the entrance and a blue-grey miniature greyhound strutted into the ring.

"Now we have the winner of the toy group. Rocco, an Italian greyhound is handled by Maria Ricci. Maria is a regular visitor to Woofs and this is Rocco's second time in the Best of Show competition. Let's hope it is the second time lucky for this stunning little chap. This little dog has won a lot of hearts with his sheer presence."

A cheer went up from the crowd.

Maria was wearing an elegant blue skirt suit, and with her black curls and high cheekbones, she looked almost aristocratic. The little dog's legs were a blur as he raced around the arena giving a performance that had the crowd cheering.

"And another one," Alice said. "Una says Maria has the worst temper. Apparently, she slapped a judge once when she wasn't picked in the lineup." Alice shrugged and shook her head.

"Wow, this really is a cut-throat business." Lola was noting all of this for she still had a feeling that Una was in trouble. She felt a hand on her arm and looked over to Tilly.

"She's nice too," Alice said. "My friend says she is great with herbal remedies and has helped her dogs on more than one occasion."

"That is good to hear," Lola said and glanced at Una. She looked fine, even if she occasionally grasped at her stomach.

"Relax, nothing is going to go wrong," Tilly said.

"Oh, no," Sassy said dropping her pizzle.

Lola looked down to see the Frenchie with her paws over her ears.

"She's jinxed it," Sassy said. "Need cuddles now."

Lola picked her up to see Rocco taking his position at the third board as the spotlight traveled back to the entrance.

Lola couldn't help but have the same feeling as Sassy. Her senses were on alert and she felt danger was close by, but why, and what? Something was wrong, she just wished she knew what.

Lola sighed, maybe she was just suffering a bout of her PTSD. Maybe nothing was wrong and she just needed to learn how to relax.

WHAT A CHOICE

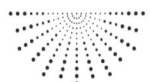

"Oh, wow, isn't she marvelous?" Alice said.

Lola's eyes were drawn back to the ring. A beagle was trotting across the blue carpet with what looked like a huge smile on her face. The cheer and buzz from the crowd said that they liked this dog and she could understand why. Her tan, white and black coat was perfectly proportioned and seemed to emphasize her beauty.

"This is Maze the beagle, the winner of the hound group and a very popular choice amongst the crowd. Maze is handled by Lauren Benton. This is Lauren's first time on the blue carpet but this team is doing a wonderful job, just look at them go."

Lola watched as Lauren trotted around the ring with her little dog. She was wearing a red skirt and a white blouse. She had long blond hair and a big smile.

"I hear she is really nice," Alice said. "The dog too, more a pet than a show dog."

That surprised Lola as they looked very professional and she could see the little dog as the winner... though, so far she had thought that every dog was the best. Maze stopped at her board and Una approached to give her scrutiny. Lola thought that her hand was shaking a little, but it was hard to tell on the big screen. Una clutching for her stomach as she turned from the dog was clear, however.

What was going on? Was she ill, or was it just nerves?

"Next into the ring is Fifi ..."

A huge cheer went up from the crowd as the spotlight was fixed on the entrance.

"... the honey-colored miniature poodle is a winner with our audience. Fifi is a 5-year-old miniature poodle and has won everything she has entered this year. The winner of the utility group earlier in the week, Fifi is handled by Mark Duncan."

"This is the favorite," Alice said.

Fifi was a delight, a bundle of highly manicured fluffy fur with a huge attitude. She strutted around the ring as if she owned it. Mark was a heavy-set man with a bald head and a deep tan and he was wearing a baby pink suit with a hot pink, much brighter shirt. When he ran around the ring, he held out his left arm with the hand turned over and swung his hips extravagantly. The dog and owner seemed to be in synch and looked in perfect harmony. Another cheer went up from the crowd, the loudest so far.

"I've heard he is very nice up until things don't go his way. Then he gets angry and it is said that he can be foul," Alice added with a sneaky grin.

"Oh, my goodness, poor Una," Tilly said. "I would not want to choose between this lot, they are all so good."

Lola cuddled onto Sassy who was watching the ring. She understood, all the dogs were magnificent and it seemed that most of the owners were equally mean. Why would anyone want to put themselves in the middle of that lot? "If they are all so horrid, why does Una do it?" Lola asked.

"Oh, Una loves it," Alice said. "Most of the handlers are fine; sure, they get a bit hot under the collar from time to time, but most of them love it as much as Una does. In her mind, she is advancing the breed every time she picks a winner."

"I can understand that," Lola said.

"Next, we have the winner of the gundog group, this is the Labrador Retriever, Queenie, who is handled by Catherine Guzman.

As the dog came into the ring, highlighted on the blue carpet by the spotlight, the buzz from the crowd stopped. The dog was clearly overweight and could hardly get into a good trot.

"Who ate all the donuts?" Sassy asked.

Catherine looked nervous. She had shoulder-length black hair that was pinned up on her left side but fell across her face on the right, as she ran around the ring. She was also a little plump and was wearing a purple skirt suit that emphasized her excess weight rather than minimized it. It was almost as if she had put weight on since she bought the outfit and it was now too tight.

"How did that win its group?" the woman behind them said.

"It's a disgrace," her friend said, "but she is friends with the judge."

"Well, that says it all," the first woman ended with a harumph.

Queenie, the golden lab was panting heavily as they came to the third corner. Catherine was peering into the crowd rather than looking where she was going. She tripped and wheeled her arms, stumbling forward and tilting more and more. The crowd let out an oof of worry until she righted herself and continued on her way.

It took her a little longer to get to her board where both handler and dog seemed to be pleased to come to a stop. Una scrutinized them both for a moment and made a comment to her scribe.

"And now we have the last of our finalists," the compère announced with glee. "This is Thor, the wonderful German Shepherd Dog and the winner of the Pastoral group. Thor is handled today by Gunter Schmidt and he competes in police dog trials in his native Germany. Look at this dog move."

Thor was a big sable German Shepherd who covered the ground with grace and a regal attitude. His body was muscular and seemed to ripple as he reveled around the ring. Gunter was a tall man with blond hair, wearing a tan suit that matched part of the dog's coat. It seemed to draw your eye to the dog and made them look in perfect harmony. As he came to stand next to his board the dog's coat gleamed in the spotlight.

As Una stepped toward the GSD and gave her notes to Mick the buzz in the audience rose to a crescendo level. They were all anticipating the judge's decision.

"Now what happens?" Lola asked.

"Oh, now it gets exciting," Alice said leaning across. "Una will look at the individual dogs, and then run them again before making her decision."

The lights came on and Lola was blinking in the sudden brightness. Sure enough, Una was approaching the boxer. She ran her hands over each dog along the line and checked their teeth. After her appraisal, she had them run once more around the ring. All of the dogs looked magnificent except poor Queenie. The golden dog was clearly struggling and there was a heavy moan of dissent from the crowd as she made her way back to her board.

All the time Lola was watching the crowd to see if anyone was staring at Una. It was ridiculous, everyone was watching her like a hawk. Lola chuckled and decided it was time to relax.

After Una had run her hands over Thor and checked his teeth as she had with all the dogs she stepped back and watched the GSD run around the ring.

Lola was finding it so exciting, she was willing on each competitor, but felt a little sorry for Catherine. Queenie and she were clearly out of their depth.

Una walked along the dogs again. Talking to Mick and sometimes stopping at a dog. The crowd had hushed, waiting with bated breath for the announcement.

Now, Una was walking back up and down in front of the dogs, she spent a long time on the Labrador and while she was there, Lola detected that she looked nervous. At one time, she caught her staring at the entrance, or just to the side of it. Lola followed her eyes but she couldn't see any problems. Some dark-suited men were standing at the ring entrance, but the distance was too far for her to be sure if they were just watching the show, or if they were watching Una only.

Once more Una walked up the row, the crowd was now hushed, but there was a background hum of excitement. Una stopped at the boxer and then went on down the row, she walked past the red Irish terrier without pausing. Paddy McKiernan shook his head. Down the row she went, pausing at the Italian Greyhound. Maria waved her hand at the dog and it stood a little prouder.

"The excitement is building," the compère said in almost a whisper. "Who will it be?"

Una walked on. Lola was finding the whole thing so exciting. She was sitting on the edge of her seat trying to decide who would win. In her mind, it was the Italian Greyhound, and then the boxer, in third would be the poodle, but who would Una pick?

"I choose the Greyhound, how about you?" Lola whispered.

"I have to pick the boxer, just for our friend, Tyson," Tilly said.

"Me too," Sassy said.

"I think the Poodle," Alice said. "I know she's the favorite but with good reason."

In the ring, Una stopped in front of Fifi, the little honey-colored poodle. Mark Duncan preened like a peacock, his left hand holding the lead, his right hand held out, it made him look a little like a teapot.

Una walked on, she stopped in front of the Labrador. Even from this distance, Lola could tell that Catherine, the dog's owner, and handler was nervous. She was fiddling with her hair, trying to tuck the one side behind her ear and then twiddling the lead. She patted the dog but almost poked her in the eye. Queenie backed away and gave her an anxious look.

"Oh, dear, that will not go down well," Alice said. "This is not all about looks but temperament too and that dog is worried."

"So is her handler, I think her nerves are rubbing off on the dog," Lola said.

"I do believe you are right." Alice smiled. "I guess we would all be nervous under such conditions."

Una had completed her assessment and went to stand across the ring. The crowd noticed 3 new boards had been brought in while they were all concentrating on Una. A board saying no 1, was in the middle in front of the huge trophy and 2 and 3 were on either side.

"And now, what we have all been waiting for," the compère said.

Una looked across at the entrance before pointing at Queenie the Labrador and walking across the ring toward her.

A howl of dismay came from behind them as a moan escaped the whole crowd. Clearly, everyone was shocked at such a decision.

Catherine looked as if she would cry and came hesitantly forward. Una shook her hand and took her over to the board with the no 1 and stood her in front of the huge trophy. Lola noticed that the only one of the competitors to be clapping was Lauren Benton, who was handling the Beagle.

"This can't be happening!" Alice said and a similar sentiment was coming from the crowd. There were even a few hisses and boos.

Una walked over to Fifi and Mark Duncan and called him forth as second. Duncan's face was a bright crimson red. He came forward a few feet and then turned, shook his head, and walked out of the arena.

"Oh, my, this has never happened before," the compère said and his voice had raised an octave or two with shock. "Mark Duncan has left the arena and forfeited his second place. His poodle, Fifi was the favorite to win, but... we are not in the same position as the judge. Just remember, we cannot see what she sees.... Well, what a result. I imagine this is one that we will be discussing for many months," he tried to make the best of this.

Una approached the Italian greyhound next. Maria Ricci came forward but she did not look happy. This was not how Lola had expected things to go. This was supposed to be a joyous occasion for these competitors. Of course, some would be disappointed but this felt wrong, even to Lola, who knew nothing about what she was watching.

Una called Paddy McKiernan and his Red Irish Terrier in third and then indicated for the rest of the dogs to leave the ring. As Paddy was displayed on each of the screens, it was clear that he was clenching his jaw and that his face was red with anger. The camera quickly panned back to show Casey instead of her handler.

A few unhappy people were trotting out their dogs. They were shaking their heads as they went. Last to go was Gunter Schmitz with his big GSD. The man came right up to Una and stopped.

Lola felt herself stand and she almost tipped Sassy off her knee.

"Falling!"

Lola sat down. "Sorry."

Gunter was standing and staring at Una, leaning over her and the difference in their size was striking at this distance. There was anger in his expression, clearly visible on the screens, but something else... it looked almost like betrayal. For a minute Lola wondered if the trouble had been this man bribing Una to pick him. If that was the case, she had been strong enough to stand up to him. What would it mean now?

Lola pushed the thought aside, she was speculating with no evidence other than an expression on a screen under strange lighting. That was not a sensible thing to do, and yet her gut said there was trouble ahead.

The smart-suited men from around the ring were running to Una's aid and arrived just as Gunter turned and walked out. What had he said? Had he threatened her?

"That was just such a cheat," the woman behind Lola said. "Una picked her friend!"

"I never would have believed it," the other woman replied.

Lola felt as if all the air had left her. She felt exhausted as if she had run fast and hard, and she felt let down. If she felt this, what would the competitors who had spent, months, years, and even decades to get here think?

In the ring, photos were being taken of the winners but the crowd was drifting away. Many of them mumbled about the corrupt judge and how she would get what was coming to her.

AGAINST THE CROWD

*L*ola kept her eyes on the ring. Tilly and Alice were shaking their heads and lamenting over the strange results. Most of the crowd was drifting away, many of them grumbling and moaning as they made their way out of the narrow seats.

The women who had been behind them were tutting loudly. So loud that it was obvious that they wanted to be heard.

Lola turned around and smiled at them, maybe they would help her understand what had happened. They were two large women, one tall with severe black hair and red-veined cheeks. She did not return Lola's smile, in fact, she glared at her. The other was shorter but wider with mousy brown hair. Her cheeks were flushed with anger. "Una will pay for this!" the mousy woman said.

Lola tried another smile but the women still ignored her.

"You bet she will." The taller woman picked up her bag and glaring once more at Lola, followed the rest of the row out of the seats. "Never fear, someone will get their own back!"

Lola felt a little tingle of fear at that. Would they really? She looked at her friends who were still sitting there.

Alice was shaking her head. "Why would she do that?" Alice asked.

"Well, the dog won its group, it must be good enough to win." Tilly poured a cup of coffee from her flask. "Want one?" She looked at Lola and Alice, and both of them shook their heads.

Why was she drinking coffee? Lola wondered as she watched the ring.

"No, no, it wasn't," Alice said. "Catherine is a good friend of Una's and we talked about her dog just a few days ago. Both Catherine and Queenie were injured last year, just after she qualified for Woofs. Catherine knows she has been feeding her too much and giving her very little exercise. Queenie likes her food and Catherine has been spoiling her a little. She knew she had no chance, Una admitted that, even though she is her friend, Queenie could not be placed, Catherine was just glad to be here. This decision makes no sense whatsoever."

In the ring, Catherine was uncomfortable and glancing around as if Hell Hounds would appear at any moment to chase her from the arena. Could it just be nerves and a little bit of overwhelm? Lola wasn't sure. However, her Spidey senses were on full alert. Something was going on.

Lola sat and Sassy jumped up onto her knee and began watching the crowd. "Lot of snippy people." Sassy stared up at Lola and looked a little worried.

Lola curled her arms around the Frenchie as people made their way along the rows, many of them moaning about the terrible result. "Snippy?" Lola whispered in the Frenchie's ear.

"Alice says it when people are mad. They go snip, snip, snip. But I can feel the anger, it like a great lion roaring as people go past."

"Met many lions have you," she whispered into Sassy's ear.

"Seen on boxy thing." Sassy leaned back into her as if she was sitting tall to back up her statement.

Lola cuddled her a little closer. She could feel the anger too. Was this what she had sensed as danger? Had she felt some strange premonition of this? No, that was ridiculous. "Should we go and meet Una?"

"No," Alice said. "She will have to do a few interviews and have photos taken. She is meeting us in about an hour."

Lola nodded as her friends continued to discuss the merits of each dog. Like her, they knew very little about showing and were just saying what they liked.

"The red terrier was so beautiful and such a joy to watch," Tilly said.

"And the poodle, wow, it just floated around the ring," Alice added. "That coat, it looked as fluffy as a cloud."

Lola sighed, were they wrong with their assessment of the competition... if so, it appeared that everyone in the crowd was wrong too... or had Una cheated?

Down in the ring, photographs were still being taken of the winning dogs. Catherine Guzman, the lady with the portly Labrador was standing in front of the huge trophy. She looked anything but pleased. In fact, she looked afraid or at the very least worried. She was letting her hair fall over her face and glancing through it at the crowd. The photographer kept telling her to look at him, to keep still, to smile.

Catherine's hands were like little birds flapping up and down her body as she fiddled with her purple jacket, or dusted down the matching skirt. Still, she searched the crowd, what was she looking for?

The suited men were calling Una over to stand with the winners but she seemed reluctant to do so.

As she came, the man who was third stared down at her. From the big screen, Lola could see the menace in his eyes. There was real hate there. "Who is this again?"

Alice glanced at the screen. "It's Paddy McKiernan; oh, dear, he is not happy. Let's hope we don't see his famous temper."

"Surely, him coming third would mean he was not angry, after all, it's only a dog show!" Lola said.

Alice's eyes opened wide. "Only a dog show? It is these people's very lives. Many of them put everything into it. They work really hard and study breeding lines for years. It takes generations to produce the best dog, and then you have to get it in perfect condition and win shows to get here. Trust me, this is a very serious endeavor."

"I guess, but even so, why are they all so angry?" Lola asked.

Alice chuckled. "There is a lot of money at stake, a huge first prize and the endorsements and sponsorship can make someone's career. Then there is the value it adds to the kennels. The prestige of winning Woofs means that the puppies are worth so much more. Then there is pride, everyone thinks their dog is the best. Oh, there is a lot at stake and as you can see, tempers are riding high."

In the ring, Catherine had burst into tears, and Una went to her and pulled her in for a hug. Now, that was not on, surely, it would look like she was a favorite?

Catherine shoved Una away and stormed out of the ring, Queenie chasing after her.

Una was knocked violently backward and crumpled to the floor. Slowly, she stood and looked a little shocked. For a moment, she seemed unsure of what to do. One of the suited men came to her and said something. Una nodded and smiled and let him lead her over to the second and third-placed contestants.

Paddy shook his head and almost pushed her over once more, as he barged past her and walked out of the arena.

The Italian woman, who came second, posed for a photograph and then tossed her hair at Una and also walked out.

Una was left standing alone in the middle of the ring. She looked very small and vulnerable. Her head carriage was lower than before. Was this shame, or had she hurt herself in the fall?

Oh, dear, this was not good. "Will she be okay?" Lola asked.

"Don't worry, she will be fine," Alice said. "Una is strong, she will bounce back… we will help her. We will see her soon."

TEMPERS FLARE

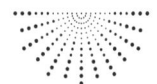

"I still think that the poodle should have won," Alice said pulling out a piece of tray bake, covered in white icing and with a cherry in the middle.

Sassy switched her attention to Alice.

"Would anyone else like some?"

Lola shook her head, but Sassy barked an enthusiastic, me, me, me. Tilly also took a piece. Once they were munching Alice shook her head. "I will be asking Una why she made such a decision." Alice broke off a little bit of the cake and gave it to Sassy without even realizing she had done it.

"I think we should talk about something else," Tilly said. "I want to watch the Hoopers later. It's the first time it has been at Woofs. Back home Tony has been practicing this with Tyson. The boxer loves it and it seems like such fun. I promised Tony I would have a look and let him know what the competition was like."

"Oh, I heard about that," Alice said as Lola felt her eyes drawn back to the ring.

The photographers had finished and were packing up their equipment. Una was talking to one of the suited men. It looked as if he was consoling her. A shout from across the ring drew his attention. He nodded at Una and walked away.

For a moment, she looked a little defeated. But across the distance, Lola could almost see her straighten her shoulders and put a smile on her face. Una walked toward the entrance.

Oh, dear!

Waiting for her were Gunter Schmitz and Mark Duncan. The tall German was angry. His hands were clenched at his sides and his shoulders were rigid. Lola could not see from here but she imagined that his jaw would be clamped tightly. Next to him, the thickset poodle handler looked just as annoyed.

When he had been in the ring, Mark had floated almost as much as his dog. He looked light on his feet, jolly and frankly harmless. The picture of him now was completely the opposite. He looked like the sort of bruiser who would be standing outside a nightclub, and maybe a rough one. There was a smaller man behind him who seemed to want to pull Mark away, but he was holding back. What was going to happen?

Lola wondered if she should go to help Una, but she would never get there in time. It wouldn't matter, Una would be fine as there were plenty of people around. Two of the suited men from the ring were standing quite close and they were also watching. They would be able to intervene before Lola could.

Una arrived before the angry reception, she raised her hand and shook her head. Her body language said that she was not interested but Gunter stepped forward and blocked her way.

Una was brought to an abrupt halt, she turned around only to find herself staring at Mark's broad chest.

The two men said something and Una dropped her head. Gunther raised his arm and Lola jumped to her feet causing Sassy to slip to the floor.

"Hey!"

The two suited men were there, guiding Una away. Gunter's body language was hard to discern but it didn't look like anger. If she had to call it, Lola would say it was shame.

Lola sat back down and Sassy jumped up on her knee. The little Frenchie reached up and kissed her on the cheek. "You okay?"

Lola pulled her eyes off the ring. The two men had shouted at each other before walking away. Hopefully, this was the end of it. But if that was so, why did Lola have such a horrid taste in her mouth?

"I'm fine, sweetie." Lola kissed the Frenchie on the top of her head.

"You could stroke me, will make you feel better." Sassy pawed at Lola's hand bringing it to the right place for strokes.

Lola chuckled and absentmindedly began to stroke. She was getting a little anxious, they seemed to have been sitting there for hours.

The next hour dragged by. Lola felt as if she should be doing something and yet, all she could do was sit here. They chatted about the competition but found that it just made them feel awful. They felt sorry for Una and were so confused about the decision Una had made.

Eventually, they started to talk about other things.

"How is your house coming on?" Alice asked.

"It is nearly complete, I should be able to move in soon," Lola said.

"We will expect a housewarming party." Tilly chuckled. "Don't look so worried, Alice and I can do all the food and you have a lot of friends in the village."

Lola felt good, she did, didn't she. It had been great moving to the UK and she was so glad that she had. "I will have to find out a date."

"We can bring some of this Cherry Bakewell tray bake," Alice said. "It is one of the few things that I make better than Tilly."

"That's your opinion." Tilly raised her eyebrows and then chuckled.

"I say it good," Sassy grumbled staring at Alice and begging for another piece.

"Oh, look at you." Alice gave the Frenchie a piece.

Sassy turned her attention to Tilly. "Maybe, I should try your version?" There was such a look of hope on her face that Tilly passed a bit over.

"Both really yummy," Sassy said.

Lola didn't have the heart to tell her that they were both the same, that only Alice had brought the tray bake today.

"Whatever happened to Linc?" Alice asked. "Are you seeing him again?"

Lola was pulled back to the present with a thump. This was not a question she wanted to answer.

Tilly chuckled. "She could be," Tilly raised her eyebrows above her round glasses and gave Lola a knowing glance. "If she ever answers his texts! Why doesn't he just call you, this texting is a little strange?"

"Oh, what have I missed?" Alice asked as she leaned across to get more of the story."

"Nothing," Lola said and turned to Tilly, "and we have spoken on the phone a couple of times. I just haven't had the time to meet up with him yet."

"Well, you must do it soon," Alice said. "He was so nice."

Lola nodded. He had been nice and she didn't know why she felt so nervous about seeing him again. After all, if it didn't work out, what had she lost?

"Why don't you make a date for next week?" Alice said. "You could go to Betty's or to the garden center for coffee and cake. That is easy and not too much of a commitment."

"That sounds like a great idea, when are you free?" Tilly asked.

Lola shrugged but Tilly raised her eyebrows once more and they fluttered above her glasses. Alice shook her head. They both knew that Lola kept her calendar on her phone and that she could check now.

Lola chuckled and pulled out her phone. "I could do it a week on Friday."

"Ha, you delayed it as long as you could," Alice said. "No more delay, do it now."

Lola swallowed down a lump of nerves.

"Go on," Tilly said and she bumped her shoulder against Lola's.

"Okay." Lola typed out a text asking Linc if he was free for an hour at 3 pm a week on Friday.

I can't wait, came back almost immediately.

Meet me at Lakeside garden center, Lola replied, and then added, *I have to go now, my friends are here.* She knew that was a cop-out, that she was delaying this too long and would probably cancel in-between time, but she had done all she felt comfortable with for one day.

"Well done," Alice said, "I'm so proud of you."

"When are we meeting Una?" Lola asked.

"I will send her another text. It should have been 20 minutes ago," Alice said. There was a worried look in her hazel eyes. A hand ran through her short blonde curls, another sign that she was worried.

"Well, should we go and meet her?" Lola asked.

"I think we should leave it a bit longer." Alice said. "Maybe the interviews are taking longer, with the controversy."

"Would you like a coffee?" Tilly asked.

"And some Cherry Bakewell?" Alice added as she had lots left.

"Thank you." Lola took one of each but she couldn't pull her mind away from the ring.

"That was in really bad taste," Lola said.

Alice looked at her piece of tray bake. "What's wrong?"

"Not this, this is delicious."

"I wouldn't know," Sassy whined a little.

"Are you sure? I say I make this better, but I'm not as good a cook as Tilly, but I love me some Cherry Bakewell. It should be moist and delicious, nutty with the decadence of the icing and then the cherry. What's not to love?"

"Alice, it is delicious, trust me." Lola took another bite and made sure that her face demonstrated how nice the tray bake was. She wasn't lying, it really was delicious.

"Still wouldn't know. Really hungry!"

Lola broke a little piece off and fed it to Sassy. Reaching down she whispered in her ear. "You're not fooling me, I saw you having some of Alice and Tilly's earlier."

Sassy chuckled and made nom nom noises.

"What I meant was the two competitors ambushing Una as she left the ring. That was really bad sportsmanship. Not very British at all!" Lola raised her eyebrows and chuckled as Tilly and Alice burst out laughing. They sometimes discussed British values and how being a good sport should be a top priority according to Tilly. Alice, on the other hand, could understand that the wish to win often came first.

"Oh, yes, that was disturbing," Tilly said.

"It was, but don't worry." Alice pointed down at the ring. "The ring team will look after Una and she has done this many times. I'm sure this is not the first or the last controversial decision she will make." Alice smiled but it didn't quite reach her eyes. She was unsure of her friend, that much was plain to see.

OH OH

"Here, have a coffee." Tilly passed the melamine cup over to Lola.

The coffee was milky and weak but it still tasted good. "That's nice. Why are you drinking coffee?"

"Oh, tea from a flask? No, thank you." Tilly shook her head as if such an idea was ridiculous. "Or from those awful polystyrene cups, oh, no, not for me."

"Why not?" Lola asked and she noticed Alice's eyes widen.

"Tea should be drunk from a China cup. The pot should be warmed before boiling water, not just hot, but boiling is poured onto the leaves. Proper loose tea mind, and it is best if it is a large leaf. None of these tea bags, uck."

"What's wrong with tea bags?" Lola asked and she could see Alice shaking her head. Tilly had always seemed quaint with her tea. Her teapot had one of those filter centerpieces that held the leaves, so if you didn't look closely you didn't realize it was not tea bags. Lola had never realized just how strongly she felt about it. The way her eyebrows were drawn down beneath her short and neat grey hair showed her strong opinions. They then popped up above her round glasses and Tilly relaxed.

"I forget you are an American. Tea should be treated with respect. Tea bags are both bleached and some now contain plastics. Plastics! Can you believe it? All the news reports about microplastics getting into the human body and they put it in tea bags which we then drink! It doesn't bear thinking about."

"I'm sure it can't be that bad," Lola said, but she stopped as Tilly glared at her.

"I'm afraid it's very true," Alice said, "McGill University in Canada did a study and found that some tea bags leak millions of these microplastic particles into our drinks. Many are sealed with plastic and they leach, but many leach these particles from the bags themselves. Once they are leached into the drink, they are then taken in by the drinker, it is awful."

"Ok, coffee it is then," Lola said with a smile. "Now, what is the plan for the rest of the day?" They had been sitting there for a couple of hours and she was getting stiff. Sassy was getting bored. She had nibbled on her pizzle, played with her octopus, and had a drink of water but it would soon be time that she needed to go outside and she was anxious to walk around the show and sniff all the things there were to sniff. Lola had promised her that she could pick out one toy and one treat. Sassy would not forget that in a hurry and was eager to be on the hunt.

"Well, Una was going to show us around the show!" Alice shrugged her shoulders. "She's late... I do hope her decision hasn't got her in any trouble."

"Of course, it won't have. The golden rule of all competition is that the judge's decision is final." Tilly nodded her head as if that was the end of it. "I could do with a walk, though. My old bones are getting a bit creaky sitting on these chairs."

Lola had to admit that the plastic, fold-down chairs were not that comfortable.

"So you think she made the right decision?" Alice asked.

"That didn't seem like the right decision, well, to me," Tilly said.

Lola tended to agree. "I don't know much about dogs and showing, but the one that won... I would have put it last."

"I would agree with you," Tilly said.

Alice let out a sigh. "I've never heard of anything like this. Una is a renowned judge and she has judged here before. I've heard of controversial decisions, that is the name of the game... but nothing like this. Nothing where she awards such a prize to, let's face it, a rather portly Labrador. Nothing that caused so much shock that a howl of dismay can be heard throughout the arena."

"And what about Mark?" Tilly asked, "Does that sort of thing happen often?"

"I have never heard of a person walking away from a reserve, especially not the reserve Best in Show at Woof's. It makes no sense whatsoever." Alice was biting her lip, clearly concerned over the outcome.

"I'm sure it will all blow over," Lola tried and gave a weak smile, it would probably blow over quicker than the plastic in the teacup.

"It wasn't a decision I expected Una to make. She's normally very fair," Alice said. "I wonder where she can be, she's usually, also, very prompt."

Sassy crawled across the space between Lola and passed Tilly to Alice. Once there she rolled onto her back waiting for a belly rub.

"Look at you, so cute." Alice leaned over to oblige pushing back the purple sleeve of her shell suit. It was a bright lavender with a big pink stripe across the middle. "You would have won the prize for your cheek."

"Cheeks pretty," Sassy said smiling even wider.

"Maybe we should go and see where she is?" Tilly asked.

"Has it been that long?" Alice checked her watch. "Oh, my, she's an hour late, something must be wrong."

"Let's go see if we can find her." Lola stood and picked up her backpack, or rucksack as it was called in these fair isles. It had been a fun morning but she was ready for some lunch. They had eaten a few bits and pieces but she felt the need for something more substantial, something that wasn't going to raise her blood sugar.

"Of course." Alice led the way and they walked along the row and out of the ring.

Sassy was determined to carry the octopus but it was so long that she was stepping on the legs and tripping herself up. Though she tried to lift her head higher to keep her prize it was no use. Lola bent down to take it, Sassy bared her teeth and growled, it was not aggressive, she thought Lola was getting down to have a game. "Not here." Lola chuckled. "We can play when we get home, release."

Sassy's eyes and mouth drooped as she let go of the toy.

"You can have it back later."

Sassy was smiling again and trotted off after Alice and Tilly as Lola shoved the octopus into her rucksack.

Alice weaved through the crowds past the rings and the benches where all the show dogs were kept in between their performances. "The room she was using is just at the end of this hall," Alice said.

They stepped aside as a pale-looking Gunter rushed past them almost colliding with Tilly. At the last moment,

Lola reached out, grabbed her arm, and pulled her to one side.

"What's his hurry?" Alice asked.

"See, no manners." Tilly smiled her thanks at Lola.

"I bitsey him if he come back," Sassy growled after the retreating German who was knocking other people over as he made his way back to the benches in great haste.

They began walking again and Sassy dropped her nose to the ground sniffing. "What is it?" Lola asked.

"Nasty plant." Sassy carried on sniffing and was pulling on her lead. She was snuffling now and blowing the scent out of her nose as fast as she sniffed it in.

Lola wanted to tell her that if it was so nasty, that she should probably stop sniffing it but she knew that wouldn't work and it was a hard conversation to have, surreptitiously. The crowd was thinner here, as it was an area where there were no stands or stalls and nothing for people to see. There were just a few offices along the back wall.

"Here we go." Alice knocked on a green door and waited for an answer. There was none. "Maybe she went to look for us." Alice shook her head. "She's not normally like this."

"Call her again," Tilly said.

Alice pulled her phone from her shell suit pocket. "She's not looked at the last message yet."

"Go on, call her." Tilly shrugged. "Texts and messages, I will never understand."

"Oh, oh," Sassy said and pawed on the door of the room.

Lola had a sinking feeling. Whatever was making Sassy worried was behind that door and it was, no doubt, the reason why Una had not met them for lunch."

Alice was holding her mobile phone, as the British called a cell, to her ear and shaking her head. "She's not answering."

Lola walked up to the door and tried the handle. It turned and as it did she wished that she had covered the handle first. If this ended up being a crime scene, she had just smudged any prints that might have been on it.

Lola pushed open the door and the scene inside took her breath away. A worried-looking dalmatian dog was curled up on the floor next to the body of Una. The floor of the small room was covered in what looked like bloody pawprints.

There had been a death at the dog show, now Lola had to find out if it was murder or if the dog had somehow caused an accident.

"Oh, my, Una!" Alice rushed into the room.

A DEATHLY DISCOVERY

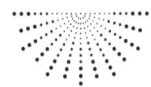

"Oh, my." Alice rushed into the room and Lola had to grab ahold of her purple shell suit to stop her from trampling over the evidence. The shiny material was slippery and Alice was moving at quite a pace, so the shell suit almost slipped through Lola's fingers. She clutched on a little harder and pulled Alice to an undignified halt.

"Let me go, she might need help!" Alice wailed.

"It's too late." Lola was sure that Una was no longer with them. "We need to preserve the scene."

"Nasty smell, night night plant," Sassy said and she sneezed.

The Dalmatian let out a plaintive whine and Sassy crossed to it. She was very careful to avoid a few footprints in the blood. When she got to the dog, she sniffed it and then curled down next to her, laying her head on the dog's shoulder.

"Needs cuddles, sad," Sassy said.

"What should we do?" Tilly asked looking at Lola.

There appeared to be no immediate danger. The room was covered in bloody paw prints, but was it? The red liquid didn't seem quite right, it was thin and there was no sign of an injury to Una.

Lola took a breath, she could look into this later, but for now, she had to help her friends. Alice didn't need to see any more of this. "Go outside and call the police." Gently, she guided Alice out of the door, preventing her from looking in any more detail. "Don't allow anyone else into the room and if anyone is standing nearby, watch them, they could be the killer.

Alice's eyes opened so wide they were just hazel dots in a sea of white. "That could be dangerous!"

"No, the killer won't come after you. I just meant if anyone is looking nervous or keeping an eye on the room, note who they are. Stay close to the door, don't worry, I am here. If anyone approaches you, call me."

"That sounds like a good plan," Tilly said and took Alice's arm.

"But... but... Una, I can't leave her, and what about Willow?"

"Who?" Lola asked but she thought she knew for the dog had lifted her head and whined once more.

"Willow is Una's dog. Her full name is Stubbana Willow in the Wind."

"Does she know you?" Lola hoped so for the dog was traumatized and it would be best to get her out of the room.

"A little." Alice pulled a gravy bone dog treat from her pocket and held it out.

Willow whined and placed her head on her paws. Sassy came around to her head and licked her face grumbling and groaning and almost barking in a way that only a Frenchie could. Only, for once it didn't make Lola smile, but it did make her proud for she could hear Sassy telling Willow that all would be okay and that they had

DEATH AT THE DOG SHOW

to leave the room so that Lola could help find out who did this.

"Did you see?" Sassy asked.

Willow's eyes were wide. "No, the man brought me back, came in and he ran."

"Who?" Lola asked.

"Who what?" Tilly asked her.

"Sorry, I was thinking aloud, who would do this?" Lola smiled and indicated for Alice to leave the room. Her friend was in shock and the sooner she got her out of there the better. She guided Willow from the room and over to Alice. It was only then that Lola realized that the dog still had a lead attached to her collar.

"Do you want me to call the police?" Lola asked as Alice looked so distraught, more so than she had ever seen her.

Alice shook her head and straightened her shoulders. "I am fine, you go back in there and find out who did this. I know she made a bad decision but she didn't deserve to die."

Lola pulled Alice into a hug and squeezed her tight. "I will find out who did this. I promise we will get justice."

As Lola went back into the room, Tilly squeezed her arm. "I will call the police and then get us some hot tea. I will keep an eye on things. Don't worry, we are both strong and we will take care of Willow."

"I know you are." Lola had to swallow for seeing her friends in such distress was affecting her too. She would find out who did this and make sure that they were punished. "Are you coming?" she asked Sassy.

The little Frenchie leaned against Willow one last time and trotted back to her. "I sniffies out clues, we catch bad man."

Lola took her back into the room and looked at the mess. "It might not be a man." Hadn't she read somewhere that poison was a woman's weapon? Then she remembered the two women behind her, they had said that Una would get her comeuppance, could they have done this?

REVIEWING THE SCENE

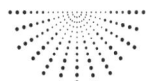

*L*ola put her rucksack down in the corner of the room and pulled her cell out of it along with some blue latex gloves that she had started keeping on her. Quickly, she took some pictures of the room and of Una.

"Sorry, Una," she said as she carefully stepped around the body. There was no sign of an injury and the bloody paw prints still looked wrong to her.

"Is this blood?" she asked Sassy.

Sassy looked at her as if she was a little dense. "Sniffies so strong you can't tell?"

Lola shook her head. "Sorry, I can't."

Sassy sighed. "Told you, is night night plant."

Lola searched her memory, she knew she had heard Sassy use that term before but she couldn't remember where.

"You know black colored berries, like potato plant." Sassy was staring at Lola as if she must understand and then she did.

"You mean deadly nightshade?"

Sassy nodded. "There is blackcurrant as well but nasty smell is night night plant."

Lola remembered now, Tilly had pointed it out to them when Tony Munch asked if it was a potato and what were the berries like to eat. She had said that it was Deadly Night Shade and if you ate the berries or the leaves you would be going night night as it was highly poisonous.

On the floor on the other side of Una was a dropped drinking bottle and on the table behind her was a bottle of blackcurrant cordial. It looked like someone had poisoned her drink, but when? Before the judging or after? Logic would say after, but who knows, maybe someone wanted to stop her from judging, or maybe that was why she had chosen Queenie. Deadly Night Shade was said to cause blurred vision and hallucinations before death. Did it cause stomach pain? Was that why she had been clutching her stomach? Was the controversial decision because she was already suffering the effects of the poison, or was it a hint, a clue? Was Una trying to tell them that Mark Duncan was the killer?

Lola knew she didn't have long as the police would soon be here and would remove her from the room. "Can you smell other people?"

"Lots!" Sassy sat down avoiding the stains on the floor. She was in her sulk pose as she wanted to help but couldn't at the moment. She would be feeling sorry for Una and for Alice, wanting to cuddle Alice or find clues. She was perched on her butt with her back legs stuck out in front of her. It made her look a little like a Buddha and to complete the pose she stuck out her bottom lip. Lola wanted to scoop her into her arms and tell her all was ok, but they didn't have time.

"Don't worry, Sassy, just sniff out as much as you can and we will think about it later."

Sassy jumped up, eager now she had a job to do. She began taking great big sniffs as she went around the room.

Lola knew how the little bulldog felt for she could see nothing that would help her in solving the crime. She didn't want to move the body so she could not be sure that it was poison, however, it seemed unlikely that it was anything else. Sassy smelling the Deadly Night Shade in the room was a big clue. How long would it be before the police worked this out?

Quickly, she took pictures of the table. There was a bag that Una used, a big pink one with a dog brush, some wet wipes, toys, and some treats in it as well as some papers and a purple hair slide.

Lola leafed through the papers and could see that there was an offer of employment in Mexico. It was for a six-figure sum and looked to be over three years. She was just flicking through more of the papers and these were from Qatar, another contract.

"Put that down."

Lola turned to see a pair of piercing blue eyes looking down at her. The man was wearing a plain black suit and a white shirt. He was tall, with a smooth bald head and a fair complexion. There was annoyance in the set of his attractive face. He was likely in his mid-fifties and wore a look of confidence, so she guessed that he loved his job. This was no tired and bored policeman going through the motions. This man wanted to catch the killer and would no doubt want her off the case.

"I'm sorry, Una is a friend of a friend and I was just trying to see if I could work out what happened."

"Really!" The widening of his eyes and shake of his head showed his disdain at such an idea. "Contaminating the scene is not helping." His voice was clipped, he was holding back his annoyance, but barely.

"I'm sorry, I'm Lola Ramsay. I have been very careful around the scene. I haven't touched anything, moved the body, or stepped in any of the evidence. I'm a private investigator who has worked with the police before." She held out her hand, pulling off the glove, for him to shake.

The man smiled but it was not a friendly gesture, he was being polite but barely. He ignored her hand. "I will ask you to leave now, we don't want you treading in this blood."

"It's not blood, it's a blackcurrant and Deadly Night Shade mixture."

His eyebrows rose and Lola realized that she had just become his number one suspect.

"Well, that's what I imagine from the scent and the bottle on the table." Lola pointed at the bottle and hoped that she had saved herself.

"Your friends wondered if this could have been an accident. If the dog could have tripped Miss Freeman... I'm not stupid. This looks like a murder..." He let the word hang and stared intently at her before smiling. "So, let me take your details." He pulled out a notebook and took her name, address, and phone number.

Lola guessed that she hadn't quite redeemed herself and that he would be looking at her closely. Her pulse had raised, it was ridiculous, she couldn't have done this, but there again, here she was skulking around the scene and telling him what the murder weapon was. Who could blame him? She no doubt looked guilty. What had she done?

WHO COULD DO THIS

*L*ola went out of the room to see Alice and Tilly talking to a uniformed policeman. They were all drinking tea, in proper cups, and the mood was relaxed and informal. Though Alice still wore a cloak of grief, the man seemed to have helped her a lot. He was a youngish man, maybe in his mid to late 20s with short brown hair and a nice smile.

Alice still looked a little shell-shocked but the PC was engaging her, it was just what she needed.

"This is PC Cronk," Tilly said, "This is the clever lady I was telling you about, Lola Ramsay, and of course, Sassy, the little dog detective."

"Miss." The PC nodded at her and smiled.

"Cronk?" Lola confirmed.

"I know, it's unusual, I was just telling Miss Trotter here, how it is the 6618th most popular surname in the UK, 18 people in every million have my esteemed name."

"Really?" Lola had expected it to be much rarer than that.

He smiled and nodded.

"What are its origins?" Alice asked.

Lola was so pleased that this man was interesting, for Alice's thirst for knowledge had taken her mind off her friend's murder, at least for a moment.

"It comes from the medieval English cranke, meaning cheerful and vigorous."

Tilly smiled. "Well, you are certainly cheerful."

He winked at her. "Vigorous as well, but we best not go into that or my DI will have my guts for garters."

Tilly chuckled. "We will take your word for it."

"Do they know who did it?" Alice was all serious again as she turned to Lola.

"It's a little early for that." Lola shrugged.

"You told the DI about all the threats and the terrible behavior of Mark Duncan, he has such a temper that one. Oh, and we saw Gunter running from her room. He must have done it." Alice turned to the PC. "Are you getting all of this down?"

PC Cronk looked a little embarrassed and pulled out his notebook.

Lola didn't have time to tell Alice that the DI was not prepared to listen before the man turned up himself.

"No need for that, Cronk," the suited detective said. "I'm sure these ladies will try and spin a merry tale, but we will be better investigating, and not listening to stories."

The PC turned a bright red and bowed his head. "Sorry, Sir."

"What is your name?" Lola asked.

He turned on her with a crocodile smile. "I'm Detective Inspector Turner. Now, can you account for your whereabouts for the last 3 hours?"

"Yes, yes, we all can," Tilly said placing herself rather protectively between Lola and the inspector.

Sassy was with her, but at the moment, she was not growling, she must not have seen him as a threat and Lola wanted to ask her why. Was the man just winding her up? Maybe he was just being awkward and didn't really think she was a suspect.

"Well?" He turned to Tilly.

"We watched the Best in Show competition and then we sat on the terraces eating nibbles and drinking coffee. We were all together, all of the time. We were all very shocked at the decision, it was not like Una and we were due to meet her for lunch, she was coming to us so we were waiting. Alice, here, sent Una a number of texts as she was late and we were getting worried, or annoyed, or maybe even both. Eventually, we came down here to see where she was. There, are you going to look into the threats now?" Tilly blinked her eyes and wagged a finger at him.

The inspector kept his face neutral and wrote in his notebook. He would make a great poker player. "Did any of you get up and go to the bathroom or anything else?" His eyes locked on Lola and then flicked back to Tilly. "Were you all in each other's view for the whole time?"

"Yes, as I said, we were," Alice said interrupting him and drawing his gaze. "Well, I went for some treats for Sassy before the competition started, but that was hours ago." Alice looked worried now and a little afraid that she would be the suspect.

"Una was still alive then," Tilly added.

"How do you know?" Turner asked.

Tilly shook her head. "The whole of the show knows... because she judged the competition, you see, so Alice couldn't have killed her before then." Tilly put a smug look on her face and folded her arms as if that closed the matter.

Alice's face dropped again. The conversation had brought Una's death back into her mind and she really looked quite pale.

Lola reached out and touched Alice and noticed that Sassy was leaning against her leg. "It's all right, Alice, You are not a suspect." Lola turned her eyes to the DI. He held her gaze for a moment and then nodded at Alice. However, he pointedly turned back and glared at Lola. He still didn't trust her.

More people were going into the room. Lola wanted to get in there and listen but she couldn't. She looked down at Sassy and then at the room. The little dog smiled and wandered over to the room. She went inside to listen, sniff and learn.

Lola knew that she might not be able to understand what the dog discovered but it was better than nothing.

The DI had turned away from them and was talking to another officer in whispers.

"Would you like a coffee?" PC Cronk asked.

"Thank you." Lola smiled her gratitude.

He reached behind himself and pulled out a cup. "Tilly told me you would prefer coffee.

Lola smiled. "You're very kind."

The DI wandered away without acknowledging them further. It seemed rude to Lola; maybe it was meant to unsettle them, maybe he would appear and bark at them some more.

"Don't worry about him," Cronk said. "He just likes to mark his patch and he would hate you investigating.

Lola's mouth opened, *how did he know?*, then she looked at Tilly and Alice, of course, they would have told him.

"Don't worry, I find it quite exciting, but there again, this is my first murder! Oh, my, I'm so sorry. I didn't mean to be excited." He looked over at Alice but she was trying to peer into the room to see what was going on.

"What is that creature doing in here?" Turner yelled. He grabbed the lead and dragged the Frenchie from the room. Only Sassy was not going to make it easy. She rolled over on her back and began rolling on the floor, putting an expression of terror on her face. The inspector was at a loss. When he pulled, he dragged her along and she squealed out her horror with an expression of such fear on her face that he stopped.

Lola wanted to chuckle but she thought better of it. Sassy loved to be dragged along on her back, but she was making sure that he felt cruel for doing so. This was a dog show, after all, if he was seen being cruel to such a small and cute dog he would never live it down. People would flock to him, and the phones would be out, and evidence of a kind he didn't want would be recorded and all over social media before he could blink. It could end the man's career and he knew it.

"Is this thing yours?" Turner barked at Lola.

"Apologies, she must have wandered off. This is a very stressful time," Lola said.

Turner looked a little abashed and Lola came to pick Sassy up.

"That showed him," Sassy whispered in her ear as Lola carried her away.

"Did you learn anything?"

"Little blood, little cut on head but me thinks it after."

"After?" Lola asked and then she understood. The injury was post-mortem and had probably happened when Una fell.

Sassy looked sad so Lola cuddled her close and kissed her head. "I understand." Sassy loved to investigate but she hated it when people died, she was very sensitive and it made her miserable.

When Lola returned to Tilly and Alice the PC had gone.

"We can go, but we have to stay close for now," Tilly said.

"We have to go and see Gunter," Alice said. "I told them he must have done it but they don't seem to care." Alice looked both sad and determined and Lola had the urge to pull her in for a cuddle.

THE GERMAN DID IT

"The German did it," Alice said as they walked through the crowd. "It had to have been Gunter, maybe Sassy can smell that he touched the bottle or something?" Alice increased her pace as they walked away. Anger had put a touch of color in her cheeks and there was a determined set to her jaw as she marched along in a way that reminded Lola of soldiers romping across the Falklands; after all, she was in England. "What should we do?" Alice asked.

Lola had no clue, she wanted to talk to Sassy but that wasn't possible at the moment. Maybe she could make the excuse that the Frenchie needed the bathroom but for now, Alice was dead set on confronting the angry

German, and Lola could understand. He looked guilty, but poison?

"Should we just say we know?" Alice said. "You know, bluff that we have evidence and hope that he confesses."

Lola wished that life could be that easy. "I think the first thing we do is find out why he was rushing away from her room." Gunter's behavior was very suspicious. When they had first seen him, they had just assumed that he was still angry and that he was just rude and arrogant. Looking back, it was obvious that he was fleeing the scene. But, would he have behaved like that if he had killed Una?

Lola knew there was no easy answer to that question. However, his behavior did not match that of a calculating killer. It was the sort of thing someone would do if they had killed in anger. A crime of passion was often unplanned, it happened unexpectedly. In this case, the perpetrator would panic. They would flee the scene, without thought of consequences. That would be their downfall, but this killer had calculated. They had used poison and had brought it with them. Even though she hated the German man's rudeness, she had a hunch that he wasn't the killer they were looking for.

"He did it, I know it!" Alice said.

However, convincing Alice might take a bit more than a hunch.

"Where would we find him and what will happen to the Dalmatian dog?" Lola asked.

"Willow has been taken back to the benches," Alice said. "One of the ring stewards took her. They are looking for someone to take care of her. Oh, what will become of her?" Alice stopped and looked totally miserable.

"I wonder if she saw anything," Lola asked, directing the question at Sassy. "Willow seems a strange name for a Dalmatian," Lola said the words without thinking.

"Her real name is Stubbana Willow in the Wind," Alice said. "That was Una's kennel prefix, Stubbana. What will become of it? All the effort and years she put into those dogs, oh, what will happen to them?"

"Do not stress," Tilly said. "Someone will take them, I'm sure of it."

"But Willow deserves someone who loves her, someone dedicated to the breed as Una was." Alice was getting so worked up that Lola wanted to pull her mind off this thread, but how?

"If only Willow could tell us what happened," Alice said.

"She could." Sassy was dancing around in front of Alice. "I ask her if you not understand." Sassy stopped jumping. "Forgot, she said not there with man."

Lola knew they had to find out which man, that could be a big help. Maybe he was the killer or maybe he had seen something. Lola knew she had to take Sassy outside soon as there was so much she wanted to ask her.

"Sassy, darling, what is it?" Alice asked. "Are you trying to make me feel better?"

Sassy barked that she would find out who killed Una but Alice just smiled and passed her down a treat. Sassy took it but she was also sad. For maybe the first time ever, the little Frenchie was not that interested in the treat. Lola tried to tell her that it was all right with her eyes but Sassy was too intent on Alice.

"Do you need to go out?" Lola asked.

"No, want to help Alice."

Lola picked her up and cuddled her close to her face. "You are such a good girl."

They were walking up and down the benches looking for Gunter. The benches were a raised platform with partitions that the dogs were kept on in-between judging. It meant that the dogs were comfortable and secure, some in crates, others just tethered to the bench. The public could look at the dogs and the owner/handlers could keep them safe and relaxed and only allow as much access as they wanted.

Lola spotted the bench with Gunter's GSD dog and was surprised to see he had Willow with him too. He was currently cuddling the spotted dog and appeared to be crying.

Alice surged forward. "You, you beast how could you?"

Gunter lifted his head, tears running down his cheeks, and his mouth fell open as he saw Alice coming toward him. "Could I?" he asked. "What?"

Alice was on him before Lola could stop her. She punched his shoulder and slapped his face. "How could you kill her?"

"I didn't, I wouldn't ever," he said cowering back into the bench. There was no more anger, but a grief that seemed strange in the circumstances.

Lola and Tilly arrived at Alice and Gunter's side. Lola could see the pain etched on Alice's face but it was Tilly who pulled her friend into a hug. "Shush now," she whispered. "Let Lola talk to him." Gradually, she pulled Alice a little away.

"Is that Una's Willow?" Lola asked.

"It is." Gunter had wiped his eyes and was trying to look composed. On the benches on either side of him, other competitors were peering at them. Mark Duncan was staring and so was Maria Ricci, whose bench was opposite Mark's and a little further down towards the restrooms.

"I want to ask you some questions," Lola said.

"What is going on?" Mark asked.

"We will talk to you soon," Lola said and turned her back to him.

For a moment, Gunter bristled. Standing, he pushed back his shoulders and stiffened his head, holding it high and proud. The stance lasted but seconds before he seemed to crumple. "Of course, anything to help Una." He sank down into a large orange circular fold-up chair. It seemed to engulf him and he suddenly looked a fraction of the man he had a moment ago.

"Sad man," Sassy said. "Really sad, not pretend sad."

Lola agreed with her, Gunter's grief was real but what did that mean?

SASSY BARES HER TEETH

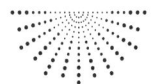

Lola decided she needed to ask Alice a few questions about Una before she questioned Gunter. The man was not acting like an acquaintance, but as if he really cared for her. The sense of loss hung on him, it was palpable. However, before she could start, DI Turner appeared.

"Gunter Schmitz?"

"That is I, have you found who killed Miss Stubbs?"

"I think I have." Turner smiled and Gunter returned the smile until he noticed the coldness in the DI's eyes.

"Come with me, you need to answer some questions." Turner pointed for Gunter to follow him.

Gunter stood and pushed the chair away. "I don't think so." Panic crossed Gunter's face and his eyes searched for refuge. They looked at the dogs. "I need to look after the dogs. I answer questions here."

"We can do that," Turner said and turned to Lola, Alice, and Tilly. "If you ladies would give us some privacy."

Lola sighed and began to step away but Gunter reached out and grabbed her arm. "You, clever PI lady that Una told me about?"

That was interesting. He had known Una well enough for her to tell him about a friend of a friend. Surely, that meant that they were more than just acquaintances. Looking at him, how he exuded grief, how he was with Willow, it was obvious, but why didn't Alice know? Lola nodded. "I am."

"You stay, help me with questions."

Lola turned her own crocodile smile on Turner then looked back at Gunter and gave him a genuine smile. "Of course."

Turner let out a discontented sigh but said nothing. They were standing in a circle now. Gunter with his back to the dogs. One hand stroking Willow. The

Dalmatian leaned into it, clearly taking comfort from him. Gunter's other hand was on Thor. It was a strange stance and made him look like a martyr on the cross.

The air between the three of them was charged, so much so that Lola expected sparks to fly.

Suddenly, Sassy was in the center of them all. She stood up on her hind legs and did a circuit, waving her paws in the air. Lola bit back a chuckle for Sassy was grumbling and groaning and looked a little like a prize fighter making her stance. "Be nice. I fightsy anyone who not nice."

"Good girl." Lola handed Sassy a fish treat from her pocket and Sassy sat on her butt facing Turner. The look on her face was one of contempt.

Turner eyed the dog and then Lola and then looked back at Sassy. It was clear that her stare was making him nervous.

Turner took his notebook out of his pocket and flicked through the pages. It was obvious that this was a delaying tactic. Lola couldn't decide whether it was to make Gunter nervous or if it was to give Turner time to get used to Sassy's stare.

The Frenchie was now grumbling away at him and Turner looked most uncomfortable. "Is she going to attack me?" he asked.

"Who?" Lola asked, enjoying the detective's discomfort.

Turner pointed at Sassy.

"Surely, you're not afraid of a little thing like Sassy?"

"Should be afraid. I bitsey his legs, or worse. I jump really high and..." Sassy let out a growl and shook her head violently from side to side. It was the terrier killing shake and it made Turner step back another pace. Lola swore that he had moisture in his eyes.

"She's fine, as long as you don't hurt us," Lola said. "Now, what questions did you have?"

Turner swallowed. "Gunter, witnesses say that you threatened Una after the competition. You raised your fist and were heard accusing her of cheating. It was clear to all that you were furious. Now, not hours later she is dead, what do you have to say to this?"

"I sorry, I regret harsh words... but the result shocked me. I lost my temper..." the look on his face changed to one of horror... "but would never hurt her. You have to understand that. I get angry, but all show, I never hit anyone... or woman... or man." Gunter looked at Lola as if asking her to verify this.

"Did anyone witness Gunter actually striking Una?" Lola asked.

"No," Turner said through gritted teeth.

"What other evidence do you have?" Lola asked.

"I'm sure we'll find evidence that he was in the room. Why were you there and where did you get the poison?" Turner turned his cold blue eyes on the German man.

"What you mean?" Gunter was shaking his head.

"What do you think I mean?"

"Don't answer that," Lola said. "I would like a word alone with my client." She didn't know if that would work, she had seen it in the movies and obviously, she wasn't a lawyer, but somehow, she felt it was important that Gunter didn't answer that question. Now, she was sure that he had been in the room, but she was also positive that he hadn't committed the murder.

The look of shock on his face when Turner mentioned poison was too real to be faked. Gunter had thought the same as they originally had, that Una had been stabbed or shot or had hit her head. He had assumed the red around her was blood. If it wasn't for Sassy, they would have thought so too.

Turner sighed. "You are not his lawyer. I do not have to give you privacy."

"Are you charging him?" Lola asked.

Turner eyed her coldly for long seconds, Sassy growled, and he shook his head. "I can wait until the evidence comes back." He leaned in close to Gunter. "Do not leave this place, stay here where I can find you." With that, he turned and walked away.

Gunter breathed a sigh of relief and sank down into his chair. This time it seemed to swallow the big man, it was as if he had shrunk down and disappeared.

"Why did you stop that?" Alice asked anger and a little betrayal clear in the pink of her cheeks.

"I don't think he did it," Lola said, and then she turned to Gunter. "If I'm going to help you I need to know everything and I need you to tell me the truth. Can you do this?"

Gunter nodded and as he did, Sassy leaped onto his knee and leaned against him, kissing his face. She gave Lola an angry look.

It was clear that the Frenchie thought he was innocent, but how could Lola prove it? For if she was right, there would soon be plenty of witnesses who had seen him flee from the scene.

MY BELOVED

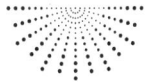

*L*ola could feel the anger coming off Alice from behind her. Turning, she smiled at her friend and walked over to her. "Trust me."

Alice shook her head, there were spots of anger, red on her cheeks, and her jaw was clenched tightly. "He was there, he was so angry and he threatened her."

Lola swallowed, she understood, but her gut said he didn't do this. The problem was, how could she explain that to Alice. Taking just a moment she let out a breath. "Look at how he is with Willow, look at how sad he is. I think there is more to this than we know."

Alice shook her head again. Her eyes were narrow, her fists clenched at her sides and tears sparkled in the corners of her eyes.

"Lola will not let him go if he did it," Tilly said. "But what if he didn't? ... you want the right person caught, don't you?"

"Of course." Alice seemed to let go of her anger... a little.

"Do not fear, if he did this we will find out." Lola took Alice's hands and squeezed them gently. The fists uncurled and relaxed and at last, her friend smiled a weak smile and nodded.

Lola wanted to tell Alice that Sassy was sitting on Gunter's knee and that she wouldn't do that if he was guilty, but she knew that would sound crazy. Sometimes, she knew it would be easier if she told her friends that she could talk to Sassy, but she also knew that, if she did, they would think she was a sandwich short of a picnic.

"Gunter, how did you know Una?" Lola asked.

The German shuffled a little in his oversized chair. "I... I... we were friends."

"How good of friends were you?"

"Good."

Lola could see that he wanted to tell her, but something was holding him back. "You need to tell me everything if I am to help you."

He dropped his head and stroked Sassy before looking back up. There was moisture in his eyes too. "It would not be appropriate for me to be in the competition if it was known how good friends we were," Gunter said, his cheeks flushed a little pink and he lowered his head once more.

"You were lovers!" Alice said.

Gunter looked up and nodded. "Una wanted to keep it quiet."

"Why didn't you call the police?" Lola asked.

Gunter dropped his head in shame. "I was so shocked that I ran. I even left Willow and that was wrong. She is traumatized and that is all my fault."

"Go back to the start," Lola said. "Why did you go to the room?"

"Una was not feeling well, even before the competition. She had a headache, and a tummy ache, and said her vision was blurred. We thought it was a migraine. She got them occasionally."

"She used to, I thought they cleared up when she went... well... after the change," Alice said.

Gunter looked a little confused. "The change."

"The menopause," Tilly said. "Is that when her migraines stopped."

Alice nodded.

"She said it was not quite a migraine but she not feel too well. She had her normal drink of blackcurrant in her bottle. You know how much she liked it, but she didn't fancy it, she said it didn't taste right and made her feel a little sick, so she only drank a little. Normally, she wouldn't drink coffee before judging but she got me to fetch her one. It was strange and risky as I had to go out and come back. I went the back way, but I could have been seen. Because of this, I knew how ill she was. I wanted her to lie down but there was no time."

"I think the poison was in that bottle," Lola said. "Who would know she drank from it and who would have access?"

Alice nodded. "Everyone knew she loved blackcurrant and that she always had her bottle with her."

"Who would have access to the bottle?" Lola asked.

Gunter looked at Alice as if afraid that she would hit him again.

"Gunter, what do you know?" Lola asked.

"Una was well known on the circuit, the room was not locked, and anyone could go there. In fact, many would have done so this morning. Many competitors have friends, they say hello to judge and give little things."

"Bribes!" Alice's eyes widened.

"No... not like that, little things... to just be nice." Gunter's cheeks were red, it was clear that the intention of these little things was to curry favor.

"You said she was unwell, was that before the competition or after?"

"Twas before," Gunter said. "She was feeling tired, and had... how you say... a growling stomach, as well as having a migraine, so she asked for a coffee. I fetched her one. She said something... I struggle to remember... I was wanting to come away, to not be seen. I knew she would not give Thor prize but... still, always hope."

"What did she say?" Lola asked and she could feel Alice and Tilly behind her who were both intent on hearing this in case it was a clue.

Gunter scratched his head, his blond hair stuck up where he had run his hands through it making him look a little like a tramp. "It was something about pressure and the foreign contracts. She wanted me to have a look at them later to see if there was a way out of them."

"Do you think the foreign men could have killed her? "Alice tapped Lola on the shoulder as she asked the question, almost as if she was reminding her to keep up.

Only Lola didn't think that the men she had seen would kill someone with poison. They were a rough-looking sort and any poison they had would no doubt be of the illegal narcotic type, not a British wildflower.

"I not know." He pulled his phone from his pocket. "She sent me contracts, digital... but then later she said no need to worry, she had it all worked out."

"Send them to me," Lola said. "You need to tell this to the police when they question you and you need to get a lawyer."

"Solicitor," Tilly said. "I can give you the details of a good one."

Lola smiled, Tilly was a font of knowledge. "Gunter, when did you go back to Una's room after the contest?"

"I was angry after results. Everyone knows that Catherine and Una are good friends. I angry twice." A look of hurt crossed his face and he folded his arms over Sassy.

"Twice?" Lola asked.

Gunter let out a long breath and Willow touched one of his cheeks while Thor licked the other. He reached out to stroke the two dogs and Sassy leaned against him. If dogs were a good judge of character, these three wanted nothing more than to give him comfort.

"Once for bad decision, more because we not allowed to be together in public as it would look wrong. Everyone knows that Catherine and Una friends, so why we not be good friends?"

"Why do you think?" Lola asked.

"Maybe she is ashamed of me..." His head fell forward and tears dropped onto his knees. "It not matter. I behave very badly. Anger too much and lose temper. Mark come to me and say we tell her, so we did as came out of ring. I called her cheat. After, I ashamed and go say sorry. She ill, iller than before. Willow had been in room for many hours; she asked me take for a walk, then we talk. I go walk Willow out of back door of her room, about 30 minutes before I found Una." Tears ran down his cheeks and he absently brushed them away. "When we came back in, Una was lying there and there was blood on her clothes and around her. I checked for a pulse but there was none and I panicked. I just dropped the lead and ran out the front. I should have gone the back way and no one would have seen me."

"You didn't call the police or an ambulance!" Alice said. "That is so cowardly."

"I was going to," he said. "I not have phone on me... there is a courtesy phone just over there." He pointed across the room and Lola spotted the phone. "Only, I knew how it would look. I was so angry with Una, I knew she would not choose me, if she did, sooner or later people would find out about us and it would be considered wrong. But, she choose her friend, a dog that could never win. I was angry, I behaved badly and I knew would be blamed for this death. I swear I didn't do it."

He stopped and reached down beside his chair coming back up with a water bottle. He took a long drink before continuing. "I watched you go into the room and come out and call the police. I was there just seconds before you. I could do nothing and I knew my beloved was dead."

SWEET RELIEF

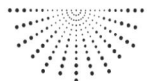

*L*ola reached out and touched Gunter's shoulder. "Send me those contracts." She showed him her number and moved away.

"I believe him and so does Sassy," Lola said before she could stop herself.

"I love Sassy but she is just with him because he is upset," Alice said, there was still an edge to her voice but not as much.

"That is right, but she also knows when someone is hiding something. If he was hiding something that bad, I'm sure she would not comfort him."

"I tend to agree with you," Tilly said. "He is distraught. Now, he could have killed her in a fit of anger, but if it is poison... that is a calculated way to kill someone. It does not ring true for a man who believes he has been shunned and cheated."

Alice let out a breath and the anger toward the German seeped out with it. She deflated a little.

"You need something substantial to eat," Tilly said, "we all do."

"I couldn't eat." Alice was shaking her head.

"No, I don't feel like it either but low blood sugar will not help us catch the killer." Tilly used a motherly tone.

Lola nodded absentmindedly. She had seen two Mexican-looking men in suits lurking at the end of the row. They were staring at Willow. Had they killed Una?"

"Do you have any other suspects?" Alice asked.

"Lots," Lola said, she pointed at the food places. "Grab us all some food, I will take Sassy for a wee and meet you. We can talk over who we think it is."

"Not need wee, wees," Sassy said and sat down in front of her. "Want to find bad killer."

Lola wanted to tell her that she needed to talk but couldn't, not in front of her friends. "Come on, Sassy Pants."

The Frenchie couldn't resist the use of her full name and had jumped up and was trotting along before she realized. "Tricked me," she said.

"Yep, we need to talk."

Once outside the hall, Lola took Sassy over to a patch of grass that ran around the back of the building. The little Frenchie was instantly sniffing.

"So many sniffies, so many dogs from so many places, lots of different food, so much to sniffy, you try!" Sassy turned to look at Lola, her face a picture of excitement and confusion. She had never really understood why Lola didn't like to sniff the grass.

This particular grass had, no doubt, been visited by a lot of dogs over the course of the show. Lola could smell that from her taller vantage point and had no wish to put her nose any closer.

Sassy gave her one last look and began sniffing again finding a spot and squatting down for a wee. "Sweet relief," she sighed.

"I thought you didn't need to go." Lola chuckled as Sassy gave her a touch of side-eye.

"Sniffies make want to go."

Lola could understand, it wasn't sniffies with her usually going anywhere in the car!

"Who did you smell in the room?" Lola asked once Sassy had finished.

The little Frenchie reluctantly lifted her nose and came to look up at Lola. "Lots, many different, some strong, some less."

"Can you tell me who?"

Sassy looked a little sad, dropping her head. "Gunter," she offered, looking a little brighter.

"Do you remember the sniffies of the women who sat behind us when we watched the show?"

Sassy scratched her ear, this was too complicated for her.

"Don't worry, try to remember what sniffies were like and if we come to anyone who was in the room, let me know."

A big grin came on Sassy's face. "Go back now, need to cuddle Alice."

* * *

When Lola found Alice and Tilly they were sitting at a table with a plate of sandwiches and more tea, in proper cups, and a coffee. Sassy went straight to Alice and leaned against her leg.

"Hello, you," Alice said before pushing her chair back and picking Sassy up. Once on her knee, Sassy leaned into her, giving what comfort she could.

"We've been talking," Alice said. "Una did tell me she had a man in her life, that he was wonderful, but she couldn't tell me any more about him. It was a few weeks ago and I had forgotten. I guess I was so excited that she was coming to judge at our little show that it slipped my mind."

"Can you think of anyone else who might have done this?" Lola asked.

Alice shook her head.

"What about the other competitors? They all looked so angry." Tilly shrugged her shoulders.

"I guess you are right. I remember you saying many of them had a temper."

Alice nodded. "Oh, they do. What about the contracts?"

Lola hadn't had a look at them yet. Gunter had sent over a pdf copy. *Were they the same as the ones in the room?* They could be, it was easier to read something of this nature on paper than on a phone. "I will have a little look but I don't really know what I'm looking for."

"We should send them to Patricia Darnell," Tilly said. "Pass me your phone and I will add her email address and a little note, you can attach them."

Lola handed the phone over. Patricia was a solicitor who had helped them in the past. "That's a great idea."

Once they were sent they were back to figuring out the suspects. "My favorite would be the thick-set bald man," Tilly said.

"Mark Duncan." Alice nodded and that fire was back in her eyes. She needed a focus to keep her mind off her friend's death.

"What about women?" Lola asked. "Poison is often a woman's tool of murder."

"Oh, I don't know." Alice was clearly searching her mind for anything that Una had said to her.

A thought came to Lola, they were assuming this was because of the show. That it was because the portly Labrador had been awarded the prestigious prize, but it might not be. "What about outside the show, were there any people who disliked her for other reasons?" Lola asked.

Alice's mouth dropped open as if she had an idea but it snapped shut just as quickly.

"You catch fly?" Sassy asked and licked Alice's cheek.

"No licky stick," Lola said and then shook her head. Her friends would think her crazy the way she talked to Sassy.

Sassy looked at her. "Alice catch fly? That how I catch fly. You never catch fly!"

Lola reached across and stroked Sassy's head. "I don't think so." She hoped the words would be understood differently by the four-legged and two-legged around the table.

"The problem is," Alice was passing Sassy a bit of her sandwich, "Una had no life outside of her dog shows. I think that is why she wasn't too upset about the loss of her pension."

Lola remembered Una saying something when she came to judge the Jubilee dog show held in the quaint village of South-Brooke. She had been conned out of her pension and was having to judge for a few years to make the money back up. That was when she explained that she had been offered a couple of contracts that made her nervous. One from some Mexicans and one from some Arabs, Lola couldn't remember the country they were from. This had to be the two contracts. Could one of these be the killer? After all, Una had been nervous and had felt a little threatened by them.

There were many places in the world where women and human rights were not at the forefront of the government's priorities. Could Una have gotten involved in something illegal? Lola's mind went straight to the drug trade, it seemed the logical place to go, but what did that say about her?

Were the organizers of these events pushing her to smuggle for them? Now, she had to find out if Sassy had smelt any drugs in the room.

MEN IN THE SHADOWS

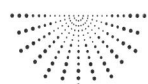

"I think we should talk to a few more of the competitors," Alice said.

"I was thinking the same, should we start with the women, maybe Catherine?" Before Lola could say any more Alice butted into the conversation.

"Catherine was her friend, she shouldn't be a suspect."

"She's not, but she might be able to give us some insight into who would do this and why." Lola smiled, Alice was fighting back her tears, how she hated to see her friend so upset.

"Sorry." The anger had gone from Alice's eyes and she looked sad and exhausted.

"Don't be." Lola's phone buzzed and she checked the email. It was from Patricia Darnell, the solicitor friend of Tilly. "Patricia says she's taking a break soon and will look over the contracts and get back to us with anything that might be pertinent."

"Good, she will spot anything unusual," Tilly said. "Now, let's go and find a killer."

"Me, I get killer." Sassy leaped off Alice's knee and was pulling on her lead, eager to hunt down the bad guys.

Lola picked her up and cuddled her, dropping behind her two friends. Holding Sassy close, she whispered in her ear, "did you smell any drugs in the room where Una died?"

"I sniffies night night, but no parrots or corpsman's candy."

Lola realized this was going to be harder than she expected. Sassy had used the British nickname for Tylenol, known as paracetamol or sometimes parrots in the UK, and her military nickname for Advil known as Ibuprofen in the UK. What she actually wanted to know, was if there had been any trace of illicit drugs at the scene. Sassy would be able to smell them but how did she explain it to her?

They were already walking along the benches so she decided to leave it until later. That was when she saw the Mexican men standing at the edge of the crowd. There were two of them, the same ones she had seen earlier and they were watching the benches. They were closer this time and she could see that one of them had a neatly trimmed goatee. He looked a little anxious, which negated her earlier view of them. As a crowd pushed past and he was bumped, his eyes were wide and fearful. The man beside him spoke and goatee closed his eyes and let out a breath before staring back at the benches.

Seeing her look in their direction, they looked away too quickly, not casually. If they had just been glancing at the benches out of general interest then they would not have spotted her and turned away so abruptly.

Lola knew she had to talk to them, but how?

Each of the benches held a dog or several and they were now in the gundog section. Lots of Labrador Retrievers of all colors, golden, black, and chocolate lined the benches. Each bench was also covered with cards, pictures, little toys, and all sorts of mementos. It looked like these were good luck wishes and cards sent by supporters. Handlers were sitting with their dogs, grooming them, talking to the crowd or some were slumped in a chair and looked to be asleep. Lola imagined that the stress of the show had worn a few out.

Catherine would be at the end of this row as her dog had won the Best of Breed as well as the Best in Show. Her bench would be with the other group winners. Lola walked along and then casually looked back. The two men had gone.

"There is Catherine," Alice said pointing. "I should have come earlier and said sorry."

Catherine was sitting in a chair staring into space. A few people were taking photos of Queenie with their phones and trying to get near her but Catherine was positioned herself so she couldn't be touched. The dog's head was down, she was clearly as unhappy as her owner.

Alice touched Catherine's shoulder and the woman jumped up with a shriek. Her eyes were red and tears stained her face. Tilly tutted and chased the looky-loos away giving them all some space.

"I'm so sorry," Alice said pulling Catherine in for a hug.

The woman looked stiff and uncomfortable in her arms. "How did this happen?" she said as Alice pulled away.

Sassy went up to Catherine and pawed at her leg. The woman looked down. "Where did you come from?" There was concern on her face.

"She's my service dog, she feels your pain and wants to help."

"Nothing can help me, I... I don't know how this happened, how can she be dead? Why did it happen after judging, it makes no sense that she's dead. I just... I just don't believe it." Tears were streaming down Catherine's face and she was sobbing into a damp and rumpled handkerchief as the words seemed to pour out of her.

Alice put a hand on her shoulder. "There, there, it will all be all right." She passed her a clean handkerchief.

Catherine was clearly distraught but her comment made Lola think. Did someone have a reason to kill Una before the judging took place? After all, Gunter had said she had felt ill before and hadn't finished her drink because of that. Had she already been poisoned? If so, this might not be about the result of the show, it could be about something else entirely, but what?

"Lady was in room," Sassy said.

Lola understood, Catherine and Una were friends; of course, she had been in there but it meant that Sassy could understand and let her know if anyone else had been in there.

Lola felt the hairs on the back of her neck crawling and she glanced around casually. The Mexican-looking men were back. They were staring at her, or Catherine, or any of them. Could they be a threat to her friends?

"Death never makes sense," Lola said. "Can you tell us a little about Una's last few days? Did anything out of the ordinary happen?"

Catherine dabbed at her eyes and reached out and patted Queenie before offering the dog a couple of dog biscuits. Queenie licked her lips. For a moment, Lola thought she wouldn't take them but then she did. Was the dog eating for comfort?

"Not that I can think of. I know she was seeing someone, but no one knew who it was. Usually, we told each other everything, but she had become very cagey over the last few months. At one time, I wondered if she had fallen out with me. However, she was excited about some job offer but I don't know much about it."

Catherine almost spat out the words about the offer. She may not know much about it but Lola was sure she disapproved and Sassy had moved to stare at her.

"We hadn't talked much because I was in the finals." Catherine gave an apologetic shrug. "It would look wrong, so after I won the group on Monday we didn't talk much at all. She congratulated me and then we only spoke when we had to."

There was something about, 'when we had to', that Lola wanted to ask more about. And, if that was the case then why had Catherine been in Una's room? Lola thought about asking but felt it would upset her more and they were friends, apart from which, she could feel the men behind her and knew it was time to see what they were up to. Could she sneak up on them?

Lola squatted down and moved so that she was behind the crowd of people trying to look at Queenie. From there she stepped behind the bench and around the back and melted into the crowd.

"Where we going?" Sassy asked.

Of course, her friend had followed. "We're going to see the two men watching us. We need to sneak up on them."

"Like I sneak up on squirrels?" Sassy had a delighted look in her eyes.

"A bit quieter than that."

Sassy looked confused, the problem was, when she saw a squirrel or a bird she wanted to catch, she let out a squeal of anticipation. Nothing sounded quite as alarming as a Frenchie squeal. If she did that now the whole venue would know she was coming.

"When I asked about drug smells I meant naughty drugs, the ones the police catch people for."

"Happy drugs?" Sassy asked.

"Yes, but stronger than those that Sam's friend used to use."

"Ok, I not sniffy any in the room. I keep doing sniffies for them." She took in a big sniff. "Not here."

"When we get to the men, tell me what they sniffy of."

"Will do."

"Now, be careful, we don't want them to see us."

Sassy dropped down onto the ground and began to commando crawl after Lola.

"You should do this, no one see you then."

Lola chuckled, the Frenchie looked so cute and a few people were laughing at her antics, however, she was convinced that she was invisible.

Lola kept one eye on Sassy and the other on the Mexicans. They were still watching the bench where Catherine and her friends were. They didn't appear to know that she had moved but if the crowd around Queenie cleared, then they would.

Lola increased her pace.

"Can't crawl that fast," Sassy said, shuffling along the floor as quickly as she could until she shuffled into a dropped French Fry or chip as the British called them. Funnily enough, their chips were called crisps, at times it was confusing.

Sassy gobbled down the fry and then chased after Lola who was approaching the two men from behind. They still hadn't seen her and she held her breath as she stepped in front of them. "Hello, guys."

THE PARTNERS

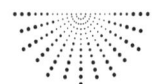

"You!" The one with the goatee almost jumped out of his skin. Maybe she had been wrong about him or maybe they came from a place where such an encounter often ended in bloodshed.

"What do you want?" The other man asked, he had a dimple on his chin.

"I was going to ask you the same thing."

Sassy was sniffing their legs and feet making quite a lot of noise as she took big breaths and then blew out before taking another.

"What is that dog doing?" Goatee asked.

"Not here," Sassy said. "Smells of dogs, Queenie, and spicy food." Sassy moved on to the next one. "Stood in some chicken, smells yummy on shoe, but no happy drugs." She sat down in front of Lola looking pleased with herself.

"She's a dog, she's just sniffing, that's what dogs do," Lola said as she handed down a treat. What did this mean? Just because they didn't smell of drugs didn't mean they weren't trying to force Una to smuggle for them.

"Why were you following Una and why were you staring at my friends?" Lola asked.

"Who are you?" Goatee asked.

Lola decided that she might as well tell them. "I'm Lola Ramsay and a friend of Una's, I'm investigating her murder."

"Murder!" Goatee's eyes widened. "We heard she fell."

"What are your names and what is your interest in her and us?"

Goatee sighed. "I'm Raoul Henriquez and my friend is Felix Clavel. We own Henvel Perros de Caza and we are here to learn about dogs." He was finding it hard to hold her gaze and was shifting on his feet. "We wanted Una to come and judge at a show in Mexico City and to help us find some dogs to take back with us. That is all, maybe we should go."

"We cannot leave," Felix said.

Raoul turned his eyes on him, a glance warning him to keep quiet.

"We still want dogs, it is sad about Una but we still need a judge and dogs before we go home."

Raoul relaxed. "Yes, he is right. Excuse us, we must talk to the other owners."

The two men walked away.

"They hiding something, little beard especially nervous," Sassy said.

Lola had felt the same thing but their story made sense. The name they had given her sounded like a kennel name as many of the breeders had. Henvel was obviously a mix of Henrique and Clavel and the rest of it meant gun dogs in Spanish.

Were they nervous about being in a foreign country and getting involved in a murder investigation or were they nervous because they were involved?

Lola watched the two men walk away. Raoul was not happy in the crowd, trying to keep people at bay. This tactic only seemed to make him a target and he struggled as a crowd enclosed around him. When it cleared, they made it over to the gundog benches and began to walk along them, glancing at dogs, then stopping and talking to one of the owners. They checked back to see if she was looking and occasionally glanced over at the bench where Alice and Tilly were. Were they looking at her friends or at Catherine? Lola couldn't tell but somehow she thought it was important.

As she made her way back, she couldn't decide if they were involved. Raoul had seemed genuinely surprised when she said Una had been murdered, but he could have been acting. She knew that you could never take a suspect's reaction as given. So now, all she had to do was work out if they had the motive to kill Una. Could it still be drugs or were they really just looking for some dogs?

"You think too much," Sassy said. "I heard brains need sugar." She was wagging her little stump as they passed a stall selling cupcakes.

"Do you mean my brain or yours?" Lola asked.

Sassy's mouth dropped open as she pretended she was insulted.

Lola arrived back at the benches. "Did you find anything out?" she asked Tilly.

"No, Alice and Catherine have been swapping memories and getting a little upset. How about you?"

"Maybe the men knew Una; they seem legit but who knows?"

THE BEST BOXER

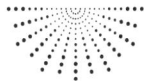

"Who are you going to talk to next?" Tilly asked.

Lola had no idea, it seemed that everyone had a reason to kill Una. All of the competitors were angry with her. It could still be Gunter, it could be the mysterious men… she didn't know who it was, but she had to decide who to talk to next. Time was short for the show only had a few more hours and the police would let people go after that.

Looking down, she wondered if Sassy had any insights for her. The little Frenchie was rolling on her back with her legs waving in the air. Her jowls were flopping open, her pink tongue lolling out of purple lips. It was a delightful sight, no use for the investigation, but it boosted Lola. It made her smile and sometimes you needed to smile.

"What is she doing?" Tilly asked.

"She hates the harness and is trying to rub it off." Lola bent down and rubbed the Frenchie's stomach. The little belly was full of too many treats and felt quite large but still, it made her chuckle. If only life was this easy!

Lola stood up, that was it, she had to make life that easy. We spend too much time worrying about this and that. Many of the things we panic about mean nothing 10 years later, and yet we let them destroy our now. Dogs were never like that. They lived in the moment, and most of them enjoyed that moment to the fullest.

"We may as well talk to people in the order they came into the ring," Lola said. "Come, someone has to know something."

"I'm going to stay here with Catherine," Alice said. "It is so nice to go back over all our memories."

Lola reached out and squeezed her arm. "Let me know if either of you thinks of anything."

Catherine nodded, she still looked so stunned, almost worse than Alice.

"So, Peter Bower first," Tilly said. "I believe he is over this way."

"Do you remember what Alice said about him?"

"Has temper," Sassy said trotting along in front of them. She had already spotted the boxer and was on her way to investigate.

"I believe she said he had a temper," Tilly said, "though, if I remember rightly, she said that about almost all of the competitors."

"It does seem to be a volatile group." Lola smiled as they arrived in front of Peter.

There was a crowd around Peter's benches. Sassy worked her way through them while Lola and Tilly stayed back. There were three brindle boxers on his benches and all were very popular with the people. Peter was supervising photos and even allowed some of the children to stroke the dogs.

"Can I have a selfie with Big Bruce?" a little red-headed girl asked. She was twizzling her twin ponytails and gave him her cutest gap-toothed smile.

Peter smiled. "Is he your favorite?"

Her face lit up in an even bigger smile and she nodded so vigorously that she would almost cause whiplash.

He indicated for her to sit on the edge of the bench. Bruce sat next to her and let her put her arm around him. Peter waved his hand and the dog's huge head moved down as if to kiss her. The girl giggled with delight and hugged him tightly.

A picture was taken and then she kissed the big dog's cheek and another picture. After a few more pictures were taken, the crowd began to thin.

"Hey, what are you doing?" Peter asked when he saw Sassy jump up onto the bench and sit next to Bruce.

"She's mine," Lola said. "Don't worry, she's fine."

Peter looked a little annoyed but said nothing more. Sassy was sniffing Bruce, checking for clues. "Did your man kill Una?" Sassy asked.

Bruce sat up a little taller and then barked at her. It was a huge bark and from such a big head it made Lola worry. The boxer could snap Sassy in two if it wanted to. The bark, however, had been a denial. Sassy was now leaning against the dog in an apology.

Of course, it meant nothing. The dogs stayed on the benches unless they were being exercised or competing. Bruce would not know if Peter had left and committed the deed.

"How did you feel about Una?" Lola asked Peter.

He looked a little confused and shook his head. "She's a great judge."

"What did you think of her decision?"

He smiled but there was no malice there. "I guess the same as most people."

Lola felt her pulse kick up a little. Was he being awkward, maybe hiding something? Glancing around she could see that his bench was very untidy. There were three leather bags, all of which were spilling equipment, clothes, leads, treats, etc. all over the area. There were cards and mementos of good luck pinned to the back of the benches but they were untidy, falling off, and haphazard. If he had the poison, it was most likely in this mess and would not be easy to find.

Lola looked at Sassy and tried to indicate for her to search but she was still leaning against Bruce.

"Did it make you angry?" Lola asked, and as she did, she noticed 2 of the Arab men she had seen earlier. They were lurking behind the benches, whispering together. What were they doing?

"Why would it make me angry?" He shrugged. "We were not even a favorite to win the group, that was the Siberian Husky." He reached over and patted Bruce. "I know my boy's good, I have the best boxer in years with this man. I'm more than pleased to have won the group and got into the final. I think the winner was a bit of a joke... but it's no skin off my nose."

"But what about the endorsements you will have missed out on?" Lola was going to push him even though his answer seemed genuine and even though she wanted to, she could detect no sense of deceit from him.

"I'll get plenty of endorsements. The first boxer to make the final in years. I'm very happy with how things went. In fact, I'm over the moon. My little man did me proud."

Lola nodded. *Little!*

"Why are you asking?"

Peter looked genuinely curious. Had the news of Una's death not spread yet? If that was so, then she could use that.

"I'm writing for a magazine and we want people's opinion of the result. Do you mind if I take a few pictures?" she asked, waving her phone.

"Not at all."

Lola picked Sassy up and whispered in her ear. "Check his things for poison."

Sassy let out a squeal of anticipation. She loved to help and loved to sniff things out. Lola put her down and as Lola pretended to be taking pictures of Bruce and Peter and the two together Sassy searched the mess on the floor. She was taking great big sniffies and then blowing the scent out to clear her nose for the next sniff. She didn't need to work like this, but it made her feel important and Lola wasn't going to stop her.

Sassy stopped and sat in front of Lola. She was holding a pair of socks in her mouth and Lola had to stop herself from chuckling.

"It not him," Sassy said. "No poison and very nice socks, sweaty and still warm. Me keeps."

"What is she doing?" Peter asked as he reached down and snatched the socks from Sassy.

The little Frenchie jumped up but couldn't reach them. Peter was standing there, with his dirty socks clasped to his chest, as the Frenchie launched herself at them.

"Sorry, she likes socks. Thanks for your time." Lola smiled at him, picked Sassy up, and walked away along the benches.

"Let me get them. If you hold I can reach," Sassy said reaching around and almost wiggling out of Lola's arms.

"Another time." She looked up and glanced around, but the Arab men were gone. There was something about them that set her pulse on edge. Were they up to no good or were they just a reminder of troubles best left in her past?

ANGRY TERRIER

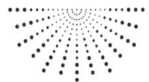

*L*ola, Tilly, and Sassy made their way along the benches.

"We didn't really get anywhere with Peter Bower," Tilly said.

"We learned more than you might think." Lola smiled.

"Do tell?"

"Has great socks, should go back and check for more!" Sassy said as Lola put her down but kept a firm hold on her lead.

"For a start, it looks like the news of Una's death is not widespread, as of yet. That could give us a clue. If someone knows, then how did they find out? However, that said, I don't think Peter is a suspect."

"I wouldn't want to rule him out so quickly." Tilly had drawn her eyebrows down as if she was deep in thought.

"He not killer," Sassy said. "He nice man and happy, too happy to have done bad thing."

Lola understood. What Sassy was saying, was that Peter would not be able to control his emotions as well as he had if he had recently killed. He would not be as relaxed as he was. It was not an exact science, that the little dog used, but it was highly reliable — unless, of course, the killer was a sociopath. In that case, they could hide their emotions, or should she say, wouldn't have any emotion following the heinous event.

They had arrived at the bench of the Red Irish Terrier and Paddy McKiernan. Lola had really enjoyed the little terrier's performance but she seemed to be a little snappy with the crowds.

As people reached out to take selfies, the terrier squared up to them, snapping and growling, causing them to jump back and scuttle away. Paddy seemed pleased with this reaction. He was sitting in front of her, brooding and almost growling at the crowds as much as his dog.

Lola loosened Sassy's lead and the little Frenchie begin her investigation of the benches and the area around them. Hopefully, she wouldn't be distracted by socks this time.

Lola hadn't taken a lot of notice of Mr. McKiernan when he was showing the dog. He was wearing a brown suit and was short and a little heavy; alongside the athletic-looking terrier he was a distraction but he clearly understood. Whereas other handlers were wearing their finery, drawing the eye of the judge from their dogs to them, Paddy was in drab clothes that made you want to look past him and at his dog. It worked well.

"What did you think of the result?" Lola asked.

Paddy's eyes flashed at her as he raised his head. For a moment, she thought he would stand, that he might even come at her for his fists were raised in front of him.

"I said my piece, dat woman cheated. We all know it."

The accent was heavy but Lola managed to understand him despite the speed with which he spoke. "I guess she deserves everything she gets." Lola smiled at him hoping to get some feeling of friendship as Sassy took big sniffs in his bag.

"Aye, she does. The likes of her will get their comeuppance, I swear it."

"You were heard threatening her after the competition. Can you account for your whereabouts both before and after judging?" Tilly asked.

Lola hadn't wanted to be quite so abrupt, but she would run with this.

"I cannae, why should I?" He rubbed a hand through his red hair and stood. "What is going on here?"

Lola could see that other people were starting to look at them. The Irish man was angry and volatile. It was not beyond the realms of possibility that he had killed Una. However, Lola doubted he would have poisoned her. "Someone hurt Una, I'm investigating and would like to know where you were between 9 and 10 this morning," Lola said.

Paddy came closer to her, his face was red and lined with veins and he was almost eye to eye, chest to chest. The man wore a heavy musk aftershave that made her eyes water and there was a touch of a smell on his breath, Guinness. Had he been drinking? Lola felt Sassy get between them. She jumped up and bounced on his knees. The angry man stumbled back and cursed.

"What?!"

He raised his fists and then saw Sassy. The anger melted from his face and he looked like everyone's favorite uncle, albeit, an uncle with red-veined cheeks from too many afternoons at the pub.

"Well, aren't ye a cutie pie?" His whole demeanor changed and he dropped to his knees to stroke her. "Look, I was angry. My Casey is a fine dog. The best I've ever bred. This was my chance fer I willnae breed another as fine but I wouldnae of hurt Una. Gunter would never let me."

"You knew about her and Gunter?" Lola asked.

"Aye, we were friends. We spend a lot of time with the same group of people. We all travel to the same shows. Una thought she kept it private but ye can't hide happiness. Twas nauseating how Gunter grinned after seeing her and it didnae take long to work out that her grin was just as wide. What did they do, give her tummy ache?"

Lola nodded, deciding not to tell him that it was a murder investigation.

"If ye want to know who hurt Una it would be Maria. That lady has a temper. Aye, she put Broom in my tea once. I had the runs all morning. It cost me the competition."

"What is Broom?" Lola asked.

"It's a plant, a spindly stalky thing, often has yellow or pink flowers. It makes you run to the loo, a lot."

"So, Maria is a herbalist is she?"

Paddy shook his head. "I doonae know about dat, but she's a witch with the herbs. Upset her and ye'll be puking yer guts out. I imagine she was pretty mad with Una. Her little dog had a good chance… not as good as my Casey, but still, good." He sank back down into his chair.

"So where were you before judging?"

"Did ye not listen. It twas not me and I don't have to answer to the likes of ye." Folding his arms he reached over to his bench and grabbed a leather hat. Placing that on his head he pulled it over his eyes and relaxed back down. They were getting no more out of him.

Lola picked Sassy up and whispered in her ear. "Can you smell night night?"

"No, not him, he nice, gives nice strokes."

Lola kissed her on the top of her head before putting her down. She didn't think it was the Irish man either. If he had killed Una it would have been more violent, much more sudden than poison. It did look like he had given them another suspect though. If Maria had used a plant to make him ill, then she could easily be the killer.

THE TEXT

*A*s Lola, Tilly, and Sassy made their way along the benches Lola's phone tinkled to say that she had a message. She checked it but put the phone back in her pocket.

"Who keeps messaging you?" Tilly asked.

"It's nothing."

"Don't do this to me." Tilly touched her arm and stopped her. "I can see that it is causing you some stress. Surely, we are good enough friends that you can talk to me about such things."

Lola sighed. "It's Linc."

"The man you met at the spa?"

Lola nodded.

Tilly squeezed her arm. "Why are you avoiding his call… message?"

Lola wanted to say… because it was dangerous. Every man she got attached to either betrayed her or ended up dead. She didn't want to go through that again. Linc seemed like a nice man, but what did she know about him? Nothing, and if she let her guard down, then something bad would happen. "I don't have the time for him right now."

"Then tell him you are busy and arrange a time to meet in a few days," Tilly said.

Lola hated how her friend was so logical, but she didn't want to risk it, not now, not yet.

"Unless, of course, it is something different that is holding you back." Tilly's eyes widened behind her round glasses. "Unless you are afraid of opening your heart."

"Of course, not." Lola shook her head to emphasize the point.

"I don't know. I think you look afraid." Tilly had one eyebrow raised.

"Moley telling you good," Sassy said. The Frenchie was staring up at Lola.

"Don't you encourage her," Lola said. She wondered what Tilly would do if she knew the little dog called her Moley? She would probably be pleased that she warranted a special name, but that wasn't helping.

Lola turned her eyes onto Tilly; she really did look like a mole as she wrinkled her nose and peered through her round glasses.

"Talk to the man," Tilly said. "It is only fair and he was very nice, very handsome, what do you have to worry about?"

Lola felt a tug of pain in her chest as she remembered another man she had cared to love and remembered that he was gone. Killed in Afghanistan.

"I'm not suggesting a marriage," Tilly said, bringing Lola back to the present. "Maybe just go for a coffee."

Lola nodded and pulled out her phone. Quickly she typed a text.

Sorry, I'm out for the day with Tilly and Alice.
How about we meet for a coffee one day next week.
I will message you when I know what day I will be free.

Almost instantly a text came back.

*I look forward to that.
Linc.*

"Happy?" Lola asked, showing Tilly the phone.

"Yes, but I want you to talk to me about this sometime."

Lola was frustrated. Her eyes glanced up to avoid Tilly's and looked straight at the Arab men. So they didn't realize she was aware of them she pulled her own gaze back to Tilly.

"I know, not today, let's go and solve the murder." Tilly smiled and squeezed her arm for support.

Lola nodded, she had noticed that the Arab men were once more staring at the benches. "Just hang around here for a moment," Lola said. "I want to go check something."

Tilly nodded and began to look at one of the stands. It was selling lots of raw dog treats and Sassy was reluctant to follow Lola. "I stay, help Tilly." Her big amber eyes were sad and her little nose was sniffing the air.

"Sassy, come," Lola called and reluctantly the little Frenchie followed her.

"You no fun."

"I will get you something later, but you have eaten too much today."

Sassy dropped her butt to the floor becoming a dead weight on the lead and when Lola looked back her bottom lip was out.

"Not eaten too much, hungry."

"You're always hungry."

"Not, always hungry, just hungry when hungry... or when lovely sniffies."

"I need your sniffies. I want you to investigate the benches when we go to them. Let me know if you sniffy night night or anything that is out of order."

"What out of order?" Sassy was looking worried and she let out a big yawn. It was a sign of stress, called displacement behavior, it took her mind off the fact that she didn't understand.

The problem was, that Lola didn't really know what she was looking for, so she couldn't put it any better, or in a way her little pal would understand. "How about if you sniffy anything from other people."

"I understand. If one people steal toy from other people. I sniffies and find out."

Lola reached down and rubbed her between her ears, it would have to do. Lola made her way across the open space between the stalls around the benches. The Arab men were still staring at the dogs, at Willow, she thought. Gunter was sitting on his bench with his arms around the two dogs. He looked despondent, certainly not like a killer.

Lola decided to leave the Arabs for now and go and see Gunter first. Tilly was still watching her and had moved away from the stall, coming closer. She should have known it would be hard to keep her friend out of this, so she indicated for Tilly to follow.

"You think those men are up to no good?" Tilly asked.

"They are staring a lot, let's go and talk to Gunter again." They wandered along to his bench. He was sitting and looking quite despondent, unaware of everything around him.

"How are you doing?" she asked.

The big German raised his head and there was a tear in his eye. "It is hard."

"I understand, have you had any more thoughts on who could do this?"

"Any of the competitors, they would do this." He shrugged. "I don't really know, but I did see a man take a bottle of champagne into her room last night, while his friend waited outside."

"What did he want?" Lola asked. "Do you mean here?"

"I didn't ask her and no, at the hotel. It was silly but I was jealous. I wondered if maybe she was cheating on me. If the friend stayed outside to warn her if I came to the door. Because of that, I went back to my own room. I left it about an hour and when I came back they were gone."

"What did they look like?"

"I couldn't see their faces... they wore Arab robes and a head covering."

"Do you see them behind me?"

Gunter glanced over her shoulder. "It could be them. I only saw them from behind and at a distance."

Lola's phone went off again and she let out a sigh of frustration. If Linc wouldn't leave her alone she would end this. She checked her phone and felt a flush of guilt for it was from Patricia.

Quickly she read through the notes. It looked like they were two pretty standard contracts but the one from the Mexicans included a clause that the progeny must come with Una. The sums involved were mouth-watering. It was enough money for Una to retire very comfortably, but what did it mean?

Patricia wrote that she had no idea who the progeny was and that it was not made clear what they would do if this clause was not met. It was not an either-or but strongly implied.

The second contract was from the Arabs and was written in very flowery language. Sheik Mustafa Odeh asked that Una build him a line and that she provide the dogs that he requested. Dogs that were to be listed in a document that was not included.

Patricia concluded that neither of the contracts had anything in them that looked illegal or dodgy and that she had done some research and the men all appeared to be legit.

Where did this leave them?

Was this the motive?

Did the owner of the dogs in question murder Una to prevent the terms of the contract from being fulfilled?

Just because they looked legit, it didn't mean they were!

The thoughts all crowded in Lola's mind, making her head spin, but not really helping. How did this help?

"What is it?" Gunter asked.

THE CONTRACTS

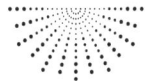

"Did Una say anything about the contracts she had with the Arab and Mexican men... anything that could have been dodgy?" Lola asked.

Gunter sighed. "I knew she was getting involved in these countries. It was not something I encouraged. I told her I had enough money we could have retired together. She could have stopped judging and have bred from Willow which was what she wanted to do... but she was stubborn and independent. We were to go through the contracts after the show, somewhere quiet, romantic." There was a look in his eye that told Lola he admired her for it.

"Where would we find out this information?" Lola asked and showed him the phone.

He read through the email and shook his head. "She kept a journal of all her appointments and all the deals she made. What dogs she thought should be bred and why and what dogs she was interested in buying. It will be in the boot of her car."

"Boot?" Lola asked and then realized that he meant the trunk. "Can we go get it?"

"It is likely that the police have already taken it, but I do have her keys. So, if they are not there, we could."

Lola could still feel the eyes of the Arab men on her. Maybe she should just go ask them? But there was something about them that made her nervous. Was it just that they were watching from a distance? Surely, if they were not up to trouble then they would have come forward? No, she would get as much information as she could before she talked to them.

"Ok, do you have someone who can look after your dogs?" Lola asked.

"I will take them with me. It will not hurt to walk them and who knows, we could use them as a distraction."

Lola agreed with that. She had been expecting Sassy but the two bigger dogs would make a big distraction.

As they left the hall they had to show a pass to say that they were allowed to take the dogs out. It was a security measure to stop someone from stealing one of the dogs.

They were going out the back way to an area where exhibitors' cars were kept and that was away from the public. Lola was aware that the Arab men were following them. Now, she was really concerned about them. It was obvious that they were up to no good.

They made their way with the three dogs to the parking area outside the building.

"That's Una's car, the blue Ford," Gunter said.

The car was sitting about halfway along the row and it didn't look as if anyone was near it.

"Would you recognize this journal?" Lola asked.

"Of course, she looked at it on most nights. I have looked at it many times with her. She was always analyzing different breeding lines and looking into health conditions. It was her biggest hobby along with judging. She thought Willow was the perfect dog and wanted to continue to improve the line by breeding her to the right dog. I don't know what will happen to her now."

"Does she have no relatives who would take it on?"

Gunter shook his head. "No, she was all alone but for Willow and me."

Lola felt a little sad as they approached the car. *Was that what would happen to her?* Gunter unlocked the car and opened the trunk. There was a bag and in it was a bottle of champagne and a card.

"Don't touch anything," Lola said.

"It doesn't matter, my prints will be on things as I helped her load the car this morning. Here," he said as he pulled the journal out of the bag."

"What are you two doing?" The voice belonged to DI Turner.

Lola took the book off Gunter behind his back and passed it to Sassy. "Go hide," she whispered.

Sassy began barking the mission-impossible tune and dropped down onto her stomach. The sound drew the DI's eyes but the boxer and the GSD jumped up and started barking as Sassy dropped into a commando crawl and dived beneath the nearest car. There was no way he could have seen her through the bigger dogs.

The two big dogs were still barking as Sassy commando crawled from one car to the next staying under it and then onto the next. Lola found herself starting to chuckle and had to bite her tongue and pull her eyes away from the Frenchie.

"Shush," Gunter said. "Easy now." He stroked the dogs and calmed them before turning back to the policeman. "I was just getting my wallet," Gunter said and reached into the car.

"What is your wallet doing in Una's car?" Turner asked.

Gunter looked at Lola and she nodded. There was no point in him trying to hide it anymore. The police would find out soon enough and if he lied about it it would only look worse.

"We were together last night... as in a couple," Gunter said.

Lola was pleased to see that Turner's mouth dropped open a little, he hadn't expected that. She also noticed, over his shoulder, that the Arab men had been approaching, but when they realized that the police were there, they went back inside the building. Should she tell Turner about them?

"I think we had better have another chat with you, Mr. Schmidt," Turner said. "Maybe you can explain why you would attack the woman you were having an affair with. Why you would talk to her in such an aggressive manner after the competition."

"I was angry," Gunter said. "I loved her, but that decision made no sense. I not kill her though. We fought at times, with hot air and angry words. I yell, I not proud, but always made up."

Lola glanced over to see that Sassy had made her way across the parking lot underneath the cars. She was lying under the furthest vehicle with the book clasped in her jaw and peeking out to see if the path was clear. She wanted to go to her, felt that it was not safe to leave her there alone, but she couldn't just walk away from the policeman.

"Perhaps, we should go back inside," Lola said. "If you have any more questions for Gunter, you should talk to him when he has a solicitor."

"There's no need," Gunter said. "I have nothing to hide."

"I left Sassy alone. Let me go get her and then I will help you."

Gunter nodded. "Sure."

Lola crossed the area sticking close to the cars. She looked back to make sure that Turner was not watching her and when she was sure he wasn't she called Sassy out. The little Frenchie was almost dragging the journal along the ground and was still doing her commando crawl. It made Lola chuckle but Sassy was convinced that she was invisible when she did this.

"I escape from him."

Lola took the book and tucked it into the back of her waistband. "You did so well."

"Me hungry, that was a lot of work." Sassy was sitting in front of her and staring with big hopeful eyes.

Lola handed down a fishy treat. Now she had to decide whether to go back to Gunter or go and read the journal. She looked at the door and the Arab men were waiting there. They no longer seemed to be hiding their interest. Should she speak to them first?

SO MANY DECISIONS

*L*ola couldn't make up her mind about who to speak to first but she didn't want to leave Gunter alone. His English was good, but he was still likely to say the wrong thing, and get himself in trouble. If that happened, who would look after his dog and Willow?

Reluctantly, she ignored the Arabs and headed back over to Gunter.

"I not kill her," Gunter said as Lola approached.

"DI Turner, I would like to be in on your questioning of Gunter."

"I see you have your dog back," Turner said and raised his eyebrows. "What show is she in?"

"She's my service dog," Lola said and pointed to the harness.

"Very funny, what can a dog like that do?"

Sassy ran at him and barked, the DI stepped back, a look of shock on his suddenly white face.

"I bitesy him where it hurts," Sassy growled and shook her head.

"She helps with my PTSD," Lola said. "Of course, some people don't understand, and some are just rude, but she helps me a lot."

Sassy was now leaning against Lola's leg and glaring at Turner.

He had the decency to look abashed and even lowered his notebook strategically.

"We would like to search your things for poison," Turner said looking back at Gunter. "Do you have any problem with that?"

Gunter looked a little concerned but Lola shook her head and gave him an encouraging smile. Sassy would have smelt it if he had the poison for she had spent a lot of time near his things.

"I guess I don't mind," he said.

"Then, let's go and search. We will be searching the car too, is there anything of yours in it?"

Gunter nodded. "Some clothes, a few books, maybe other things, I not sure. We travel together sometimes, I forget things." He handed over the keys. "You need these."

Turner took them and placed them in an evidence bag. "Let's go and see if we can find that poison."

"That would be good," Gunter said not realizing that they were expecting to find it in his things.

Lola wanted to find the killer, but she didn't think it was Gunter and neither did Sassy.

DI Turner took his time in searching through the bench and possessions of Gunter but he found nothing. He took 2 bottles away in evidence bags, but they were simply water bottles and Lola was sure that they would find nothing amiss with them. Sassy had certainly not found them suspicious.

He checked under the dog's bedding, in the bags, and under the benches. He got Gunter to empty out his pockets and asked if he had any other possessions. Gunter shook his head and looked sad.

Eventually, Turner left. "Don't leave town," he said before he walked away.

After he had gone, Gunter sank down into his chair. "Why they waste time on me?"

"Do not let it worry you," Lola said. "We will find who killed her, I promise you."

"I need a drink. A coffee to keep me going," he said.

As if on cue Tilly arrived at the bench with cups of coffee and a tray of sandwiches and treats. "I thought you could do with an energy boost," she said.

"Certainly could. Hard to do sniffies on an empty stomach," Sassy barked.

Tilly stroked the little Frenchie's head as she served the food and drink. "Don't worry, I got a little treat for you." She handed Sassy what looked like a piece of toffee.

"What is that?" Lola asked.

"It's dried yak milk, dogs love it."

Sassy was munching away on her treat as Willow and Thor eyed her with envy. A drop of drool came from Thor's mouth.

"It's good," Sassy said. "Sorry, big dogs, little dogs are best!"

Thor barked.

"What have we found out?" Tilly asked.

Lola quickly explained about the contracts and the journal.

"Have you looked at it yet?" Tilly asked.

"No, we haven't had time." Lola pulled it out of her waistband and opened the book. It made very little sense to her. There were lots of names and letters and bits and pieces that looked like English but didn't seem to say anything, perhaps it was in code? She handed it to Gunter. "Can you understand this?"

"Of course, I will have a look and let you know." He took it. "This is lines, registered dog names, they abbreviated so I might have to guess."

"What do you mean?" Lola asked.

"Well, this." He pointed to SWitW." This is Stubbana Willow in the Wind or our Willow here." He rubbed his hand over the dalmatian's head and she made a little whine. Obviously, she was still sad.

"I see, and the others?"

"These," he pointed at the lists of letters, "are health tests. Una was very keen on the fact that the dogs she bred from, would be fully health tested."

"Does it say anything about the progeny?" Lola asked, for that was what was in the contract.

"No, it doesn't, just different lines of dogs."

"Why is this here?" Lola asked seeing the word Henvel in front of a few different dogs. The dog's names were simply letters again so she couldn't work out which dogs.

"That is a kennel prefix. I don't know whose," Gunter said.

"I do. It belongs to the Mexican men who wanted Una to come out and judge." Lola had an inkling about the name but she couldn't put her finger on it. However, when she got feelings like this, it usually meant something.

"I can look into it more," Gunter said. "There are later entries with just H, we can presume that is Henvel, but these are gundogs. I know very little about them. I won't be able to work out the names, but I have a friend who will know whose dogs these are and if it means anything."

"Could they be the progeny that is mentioned in the contract?"

"They could be. Maybe their dog has sired a puppy that they want back. It is not unusual. You always try to keep the best out of the litter but at eight weeks old it is often hard to tell. Maybe, they want a dog back and the owner won't give it up."

That made sense. Lola knew that she would do anything to keep Sassy safe, maybe not commit murder, but pretty much anything. Who was she kidding, anyone who hurt her little girl would feel her wrath. The owner of this dog, the one the two men wanted, would feel much the same. Could this murder have been about saving a dog? Was Una trying to pressure someone to give up their dog? The more she looked into this the more complicated it became. What had looked like a simple case of anger, was turning out to be so much more.

THE FIERY ITALIAN HERBALIST

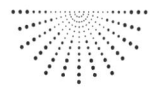

Lola left Gunter looking into the kennel names and decided to continue to question the competitors.

"What if it's a friend of the competitors, or about something totally different?" Tilly asked.

"Then I guess we're stuck," Lola said. "However, I get the feeling that we are getting closer." She couldn't explain the excitement she felt inside, even as the case began to make less and less sense. At the moment, this was at an instinctual level but she knew the answer would come, she just hoped it would be soon. Once the day was over, the competitors and everyone would disperse to the four corners of the world. Then, she would have no chance of finding the killer.

"Really! How do you know?" Tilly asked and the look on her face was not one of confidence.

"I don't know, it is just an instinct, a gut feeling, I guess. Come on, we may as well talk to Maria. Sassy, get your sniffies on, she could be the one; remember, she had given Paddy something to make him ill!"

"You are funny talking to her like that," Tilly said.

"I know, but it makes me feel better."

"Not funny, I talk," Sassy said and she sat in front of Tilly.

"Look at you, it's almost as if you can understand." Tilly chuckled and rounded Sassy to make their way along the benches.

Maria's bench was on the other side and there was no one around her. Crowds of people were still milling around the benches but it looked like they had picked a good time to come and see the Italian.

Maria was sitting very straight-backed on a tall stool and looking very aristocratic. Wearing a royal blue skirt suit, her long brown curls were cascading over her face and she appeared to be filing her elegant nails that were painted in a color that matched her suit perfectly.

"I'd like to ask you some questions about the judging," Lola said.

Maria looked up. "Non-parlo inglese." Without waiting for a reply she turned her back on them and continued filing.

"Really, that is not what I'd heard and as Una was poisoned I should probably tell the police that you have been known to poison your fellow competitors."

"Mannaggia!" Maria let out a sigh. "Ok, I talk to you. Una poisoned?! I heard she was attacked."

"Really, she was poisoned, what do you know about that?" Lola asked.

"I didn't poison her. Maybe she deserved it but I didn't do it. I'm leaving this stupid and horrid country as quickly as I can."

"That's very suspicious."

"Really, I have seen theft and murder, if my luck had not been stolen I would have won!" There was arrogance in those aristocratic eyes, and a belief in herself that was complete.

"Your luck?" Lola asked. Sassy was sniffing around her bag and under the bench.

"My lucky lead. Mark Duncan took it, I know he did. Without it, I'm not lucky."

"Is that why you poisoned Una?"

"I did not!"

Lola could see that Sassy was reaching up onto the spare bench next to Maria's dog. "What have you found?" Lola asked.

"Was night night but not here," Sassy barked.

Lola felt her pulse kick up, could have been Maria, was it that easy? Now she was annoyed that she had not come here earlier.

"Keep her away from those," Maria said. "Some are poison... but I use them to heal, nothing else."

"Do you have deadly nightshade?"

Maria nodded without there being any change in her countenance. She reached over and pulled out a black leather box, undid the latch, and flicked it open. She ran her fingers along the bottles in there, until she came to an empty space. Maria's face fell, she was genuinely surprised. "No, no, it is not here. I didn't do this, I promise. Someone stole from me, someone is blaming me."

Before Lola could say anymore DI Turner came around the corner. "What is going on here?" he asked with a smug smile on his face. PC Cronk was behind him looking very uncomfortable.

Lola looked at Maria, and somehow she believed her.

"She not do it," Sassy said.

Lola wanted to ask if there were other smells or if other people had touched the leather case. "Have you let other people use your herbs?"

"No!" Maria said as DI Turner asked her to turn around.

"Maria Ricci you are under arrest for the murder of Una Stubbs."

"I didn't do this. My bench... it is well known... anyone could have come when I was walking Rocco or visiting the powder room. Help me!"

Lola nodded, but for now, there was nothing she could do. DI Turner gave her a satisfied smirk as he gathered the herbal supplies and placed them in an evidence bag.

"It not her," Sassy said.

Tilly was too far away and so Lola picked Sassy up. "It could be, she has motive, means and the opportunity."

Sassy was shaking her head. "She nice, doggy nice and she not do this."

"How do you know?" Lola asked.

"She smells good, angry and a little bitter but not like a killer. No smell of night night on her and her feet smell nice."

Lola felt herself want to chuckle. It often boiled down to feet and socks with Sassy, but funnily enough, she was surprisingly accurate. Very rarely did a killer have socks that Sassy liked! "Well, if it's not her who is it?"

Sassy whined. "I not know, but I want to find out, liked Una and like Alice. Want to make her happy again."

THE MISSING LUCK

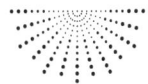

"I guess you found the right person just as the police worked it out," Tilly said.

"I don't think it was Maria," Lola said.

"But it's her poison; surely, it must be her?"

Lola didn't know what to think and she could see that Tilly was getting tired. "I don't think so, and I will keep looking for a little while longer. Do you want to go and see how Alice is for a while?"

"Do you think that's a good idea?"

"I do, have a chat with her and Catherine, see if you can find anything out and I will be along shortly for a coffee."

"A cuppa, that sounds like a plan. PC Cronk showed us a place that has proper cups. The Cottage Tea Room, it was just a little further along than where we went this morning. It was such a pleasant surprise," Tilly said and left them to walk along the benches.

Lola chuckled, it wasn't that long since they had a drink, but Tilly was always up for another.

"She smells tired, I not tired."

"You're never tired."

"Am too, sleep lots but not when sniffies to be done."

"Good, let's go and see what we can find."

They made their way along the benches to Lauren Benton. She was busily chatting with people and allowing them to take selfies with her lovely Beagle, Maize.

"Lauren, can I have a word?" Lola asked.

"Of course, would you like a picture? Oh, my, she is lovely." Lauren bent down and stroked Sassy.

"It's a little more serious than that," Lola said and she watched Lauren's face. The woman didn't even blink, but she did turn and give Lola her full attention.

"What can I help you with?"

"Did you know that Una was dead?"

Lauren's mouth dropped open with shock and tears formed in her eyes. It was too spontaneous and too instant to be anything but genuine emotion. "I'm so sorry to hear that. What happened?"

"She was poisoned."

"Oh, my goodness, how awful. Do you know who did this?"

"I'm trying to find out. What did you think of the result of the show?"

"I love Catherine and Queenie is a wonderful dog. I'm so pleased for her."

Lola could see that Sassy had stopped sniffing around the bench and was leaning against Lauren's leg. Trying to give comfort. Lola pointed to her seat and Lauren sank into it.

"You might be the only one who has that opinion," Lola said.

"Really, some of the others, they take things too seriously. It's just a dog show and yes, I love it, and yes, I work hard... but to kill! That is just crazy."

"The police think it might have been Maria, what do you think?" Lola could see that Lauren would be able to see Maria's bench from where she was, maybe she had an idea.

"No, Maria would never do this. She helped me so many times. Lent me things, helped me with paperwork, and gave me lots of advice when I was just starting. No, she would never do this. I know she was angry but not murder. No, never!"

"I heard she had poisoned Paddy, if she can do that, then why not this?"

"That was just a mistake. Paddy took a drink out of her flask, it was a remedy for one of her dogs. He thought it was whiskey and blamed her, but it was an accident and he shouldn't have done it."

Now that was interesting. Maybe Paddy was back on the suspect list. "Did you see any of the other competitors at Maria's bench over the last few days?"

Lauren thought hard. "Oh, yes, I saw Mark there last night and Catherine was looking for her... let me think... it was yesterday. We all go to each other's benches though. To ask questions, to pass on information, you know the sort of thing, so I'm sure it was nothing."

Lola wasn't so sure, but she was distracted. She could see the Arabs were still watching Gunter. It was time to find out what they were up to.

* * *

Lola went around behind the Arabs and came up to them. She was very quiet, hoping to hear them saying something but they were just watching.

"What are you doing?" she asked.

They both jumped and looked at her as if she had no right to question them. They were about to walk away when Lola reached out and grabbed the taller one's arm. His companion reacted quickly and tried to remove her hand. He was strong and trained, obviously, a bodyguard, but Lola shook him off with ease. "Ok, I have your attention, now talk to me," she said.

"I am Sheik Mustafa Odeh and this is my bodyguard, Farug Nagi, you have no right to question me." His chin was pointed up and he was refusing to look at her.

"And yet I do!"

The sheik's eyes lowered and there was shock on his face. He was not used to being spoken to in such a manner, especially by a person of the female persuasion. "Why are you watching Gunter? Did you have anything to do with Una's death?"

They both shook their heads. They looked shocked and disappointed to be asked. The sheik was in his late forties with a beard and deep brown eyes. His bodyguard was younger and kept silent.

"You'd better start talking, or I will tell the police that you have been behaving mighty suspiciously. What did you have to do with her death?"

Sassy was sniffing at their thobes. "Oh! No socks but feet sniffy good."

"Death! I would not do this. I had a deal with Una, one that I am devastated to see fall through."

He waved his leg and looked down. Seeing Sassy with her head sticking out from under his thobe, Lola felt her heart constrict. What would he do? If he tried to kick her or hurt her she was ready. She tensed for action.

The Sheik let out a peal of laughter. It was so unexpected that Lola let out a big breath of air.

"Aren't you a little cutie, now come on out of there." He reached down and in his hand was a piece of cheese. Lola had no idea where it came from for she hadn't seen him go to a pocket. Using it, he lured Sassy out from under his clothes and then into a sit. Then he stroked her and gave her the treat. "She is very nice. I like all dogs."

"I can see that." Lola smiled at him and then tried to stop it. Her reaction had been automatic, for he seemed so nice, but was it an act? "Tell me, what did you do to Una?"

"Nothing! Una and I were going to breed from Willow with my dog. We were planning on starting a new line of Royal dogs that would take the world by storm. She is dead... then now, it has all gone..." A look came on his face, a faraway look but then he focused on her and there was a smile on his face. "Unless I can persuade Gunter to let me take Willow."

"You are after the dog?" Lola asked.

"Yes, we had a contract. Una had agreed to judge but also to breed her Willow with my Falcon, my favorite dog. It would have been something great."

"Would Willow be the progeny?"

He shook his head. "No, surely, they would be the... how you say... little dogs...?"

"Puppies." Lola smiled.

"Yes, puppies." There was a sadness on his face that would be hard to fake. Of course, Una could have changed her mind and reneged on the deal. Would that be a reason for him to kill her? It could be but then... if it was what she wanted it would be in her journal. "Maybe this can still go ahead. Have you spoken to Gunter?"

"We didn't know how to go about it. We were waiting for Una to come down to the benches. She said to not approach Gunter but to wait for her to come to us. Then Farug heard that Una was dead and we didn't know what to do. I kept hoping it was wrong, that she would appear."

"That was why you looked so suspicious," Lola said. "You were hanging around waiting for her, hoping that she was not dead."

"That is right. Now, you say she is dead. We had heard this but did not believe it was true, can you help us?"

"I can introduce you to Gunter, come with me." Lola led them over to the benches. She wanted to speak to Paddy as well and find out if what Lauren said was true. If he hadn't really been poisoned but had caused it himself!

Lola lead the two men to Gunter's bench, Sassy was happily taking bits of cheese from the sheik and Lola was sure she would say these two were innocent.

"Gunter, these two had a contract with Una to breed from Willow. Can you see if it was in Una's book and if so, can I leave it with you?"

"Of course." Gunter turned to the men.

"Ok, I will continue looking for the killer, you see if you can help these two men, and let me know if you find anything that could help."

Gunter nodded and then turned to the sheik. "What is your dog's name?"

"Falcon."

Gunter began to search in the book and Lola left him to it. What now?

Lola crossed to Paddy's bench.

"What do you want now?" he asked.

"Can you explain about the broom poisoning, I have heard that this was an accident, is that true?"

Color rose on Paddy's cheeks, it was true.

"Aye, I guess it was my fault but she had the poison in a hip flask, of course, people would take a drink."

Lola felt her eyebrows raise, she would not just take a drink out of another person's hip flask without being offered it, but then, Paddy looked as if he might find such a thing too much to resist.

"Do nae judge. I was so angry that I thought she might have done it. She has all that poison. Who else could have done it?"

"I guess anyone who knew that Maria had the poison. Who would that be?"

Paddy's eyes looked so sad and his shoulders dropped. "Anyone who knew her… all of us!"

Lola nodded. He was right and she had nothing else on him. "Okay, thanks." Sassy was leaning against the man. Lola indicated for her to follow and as she looked up she saw Mark Duncan watching her. The man looked furtive and Lauren had seen him at Maria's bench.

He had a motive and the opportunity to steal the poison, but was he a cold-blooded killer?

FOUND LUCK

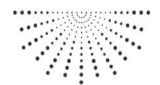

"Remember sniffies for anything out of the ordinary," Lola said as she crossed to Mark's bench with Sassy.

"Not know ordinary, what comes out of it?" Sassy said. She had sat down and was scratching her ear.

"Sorry, little girl, just sniffy out anything that doesn't belong."

Sassy still looked confused but it was too late, they were at Mark's bench. Though he had been watching her earlier, he was now pretending that he was not aware of her presence. The man's back was ramrod straight, his head held high as he talked to a member of the public about his dog.

"Fifi was the favorite, there was nothing in the class that could have beaten her," Mark said.

"We agree totally, that decision was a joke."

"It certainly was."

The crowd was definitely on his side.

"That must have made you very angry," Lola said, butting into the conversation. The two spectators turned and walked away, looking decidedly uncomfortable.

Mark turned to Lola and ran a hand over his bald head. It was a nervous gesture, but did it make him look guilty?

"And who are you?" Mark asked.

"Mark, dearest, that's confrontational. Forgive me, I'm Phillip, Mark's partner." A smaller man with dark hair and a fair complexion stood up as if from nowhere. He had a pleasant if angular face and deep brown eyes that made him look younger than Mark but Lola guessed he was the same age. Wearing a pink shirt open at the neck and blue jeans, he looked relaxed and confident. Lola couldn't help but notice that the pink of the shirt matched the color of Mark's suit.

"I'm Lola Ramsay. I'm a friend of Una's." Lola held out her hand and though Phillip was a little slow, he shook it. The handshake was firm and quick. Lola offered her hand to Mark but he shook his head.

"Mark, dearest, come on now, Una was a friend once too."

Mark sighed and shook his head and shoulders. "All right, but I'm still very angry over the decision. I believe it was all because of the Mexican deal. That was when she began to act fishy."

"In what way?" Lola asked.

"Avoiding eye contact, sneaking about, giving her friends the most prestigious award in the whole of the calendar!" Mark's mouth was drawn into a tight line, his arms crossed, his head held high.

"Tsk, tsk, Mark. Let it go," Phillip said.

Mark sighed and folded his arms across his chest in an aggressive gesture that actually made him look defensive.

Lola noticed that Sassy had found a few dog treats on the floor. She gulped them down and then looked around to see if she had been caught. Spotting that Lola had seen, she gulped. "Ooops, sorry. I sniffies for more clues."

"I have to say, you threatened Una," Lola said as she watched Sassy sniffing in his bags and around the bench, her little tail waving like a flag. She was now crawling under the bench, had she found something?

"I was not the only one." Mark unfolded his arms.

"Stop being so defensive," Phillip said. "He has not left my side except for a few trips to speak to other competitors. Even then, he was never out of my sight, not since the competition. I'm not stupid."

"What's that supposed to mean?" Mark turned on his own partner.

"I love you, but I know what you are like. I know that you would lose your temper and if you and Una were alone..." Phillip shook his head. "I dread to think what you might have done."

"I did nothing!" Mark was affronted by his partner's words and was looking away across the benches. Lola noted that his eyes were on the bench of Maria, the place he had been seen, the place where the poison had been taken.

At the moment, PC Cronk was bagging up items from Maria's bench. It looked like the police thought they had their killer.

"I'm not being disloyal." Phillip put an arm on Mark's shoulders. "Quite the opposite, I'm giving you my support, my love... as an alibi."

Mark relaxed and turned back. "I didn't do this. I heard she was poisoned... if I killed her it would have been... more direct." He was staring straight at Lola and she decided it was a good opportunity to watch his reaction.

"Then what were you doing at Maria's bench this morning?" Lola asked.

Mark's face colored instantly.

"Found it, out of ordinary," Sassy said and she came out from under the bench with a slim diamond-encrusted royal blue lead. Though it was beautiful, it was obviously old and well-used, but still, a fabulous lead. "This sniffies of Maria and Rocco."

Sassy was holding the lead proudly in her mouth. Mark tried to grab it off her but she dived back under the bench.

"What are you doing with that?" Mark asked but Sassy was hiding under the bench.

"Oh, I can't believe you did that!" Phillip said. "After everything we discussed and you are back to those silly games." He was shaking his head and there was a sad look on his face, one of almost defeat.

"What silly games?" Lola asked.

Phillip was still shaking his head and Lola thought there might be a tear in his eyes, but he turned and walked away as if in a huff.

Mark sighed and sank down onto the edge of the bench. Fifi was behind him curled up and asleep in a crate. "It was silly of me, especially when you consider the result."

Lola understood. "The lead is Maria's luck," Lola said for it made sense now. Maria's Rocco was a beautiful dog and perhaps the biggest competition to Mark's Fifi.

"I know it was wrong, stupid, and spiteful, but it's just smart competition. Maria believes she can't win without the lead. It's caused a lot of problems in the past and I was paying her back for poisoning Paddy."

"Did she poison him or did he take her drink?"

"Well, she shouldn't have poison in a drinks bottle, should she?"

Lola partly agreed with him, but this didn't help. "Can you call Phillip back?"

Mark pulled out his phone and dialed. He wouldn't meet her eyes as he waited for Phillip to answer. "I'm sorry, I'm really sorry and the lady would like to talk to you, come back. I promise I won't do it again." Mark turned to look at Lola with a smile on his face and a tear in his eye. "He's on his way."

Lola relaxed. She no longer thought that Mark was a suspect, but there was still one question that was needed to clear him. After that, maybe he could shed some light on the Mexican men and the deal they had made?

NEVER AGAIN

"Oh, my love, never again," Phillip said before taking Mark's head in his hands and planting a huge kiss on his lips. "Never cheat again."

"I promise," Mark said.

"You need to learn to channel that temper, but we can do it together." Phillip stared at him for a few more moments, before he turned to Lola. "Now, what can I do for you?" There was a guarded smile on his face.

"Well, I wanted to ask you both, if Mark was alone with Una before the competition today?"

"No, I wasn't, that would not have been acceptable," Mark said.

"I can vouch for that. We were together all morning. I was keeping his nerves in check," Phillip said.

"You are my rock, I don't know what I would do without you," Mark replied.

"Oh, I will always be here for you, as you have been for me."

"In that case, you are off the hook," Lola said. "Una was ill before the competition. The poison causes hallucinations and nausea before death. Because she was already feeling ill, Una had a coffee instead of finishing her normal drink. That is probably why she didn't die before the competition."

"You suspect that Maria's poisons were used?" Mark asked.

"I do."

He shook his head. "Maria would not make a mistake like that. If she had done this, then Una would either be ill or dead. I do not believe that Maria would kill Una, even after this," Mark waved his hands in the air and shook his head, "this travesty. But if she had, she would have done it well. She knows exactly what dose to use, for what purpose. She would not have made the mistake to make her ill and then have her die at a later time. She has used her remedies on many a dog and she always got the dose right."

That made sense. "Ok, that gives me something to think about. Who would want her dead before the competition?"

"That's the strange thing, no one." Mark was shaking his head, clearly confused.

"What do you know about the Mexican deal?" Lola asked.

"Nothing," Mark said and he looked at Phillip.

"Very little, but Catherine told me that they were trying to make something awful as a condition of her going."

"What was that?" Lola asked.

"I don't know, I can't imagine. Do you have any ideas, Markey, my love?"

"No, I don't know Catherine as well as you." Mark shrugged.

"Well, that's because you bark at people like a big angry bear." Phillip chuckled and took Mark's hand.

Lola found the two of them delightful. Mark was trying to be all mean, but Phillip saw through him. She turned her gaze on Mark. "You said she was different after the deal was made." Lola smiled, hoping she could coax some clue out of him. "Are you sure it was the Mexican deal and not the deal with the sheik?"

Mark looked confused. "She said that she had a foreign deal and I had seen the Spanish-looking men. Mexican, I guess."

"Had you seen her with the Arab men?"

"No." Mark looked to Phillip and he nodded his confirmation.

"Then the change could have been from either of the deals?" Lola asked.

Sassy was sniffing around one of the bags and trying to get into a treat container in one of them. Lola reached down and snapped the lid shut on the treats. "Not for you." She chuckled at Sassy's pouty lip.

"Was just checking them for clues," Sassy said.

Lola wanted to ask her if she would have needed to check the whole tubful but decided it would make her look a little strange. Besides, she knew the answer would be a resounding, yes.

"I guess, it could have been either," Mark said.

"Do you know anything about the deal?" Lola asked keeping one eye on Sassy who was back to searching for clues.

"No, all I know is that she was different, but I don't know why. She told us all it was very lucrative. That it would make her dreams come true but there was something that she wasn't happy about. She didn't mention it, but there was a tension in her when she spoke about it."

"I heard her talking," Phillip said. "Well, arguing. She was going to have to hurt someone and whoever she was talking to said they wouldn't let her out of it. Now I think about it, I'm sure it was the Mexicans that she was talking to, even though I couldn't see them. They were male and the voices... I don't want to seem... they sounded Mexican."

"Do you know who or what she had to hurt?" Lola asked, feeling that thrill inside that told her she was getting close.

Phillip shook his head. "No, sorry."

Lola couldn't think of any more questions and felt a little letdown. They were close but she still couldn't put things together. *Who was the killer and what was the motive?* "Okay, thank you for your help," Lola said.

"We're no longer suspects?" Phillip asked.

"Not from me." She looked down and Sassy was peeking out from under the bench, the lead once more under her paws.

Lola reached down and took it from her. "Do you want to return this... or should I?"

Mark sighed. "I'd better do it. I think I have an apology to make."

Phillip gave him a big hug. "I'm so proud of you."

Lola smiled, and the two men kissed once more as she walked away. However, this was frustrating, she was so close and yet still so far away. Who was the killer?

Lola decided to make her way back to Alice, Tilly, and Catherine and to see how they were doing. She had left Alice with Catherine for some time now and she felt a little guilty for that. Maybe, she should forget the amateur crime-solving and take her friend home? Maybe, they needed her support. Then again, she doubted her friend would want to leave until she knew who the killer was. Lola hoped she would not let her down.

"Let's go see Alice," Lola said to Sassy.

"I cuddle, make feel better," Sassy said.

"I know you will." Lola wished that life was that easy, but who knows, maybe her friends had come up with some ideas. Lola certainly needed some kind of clue, right now!

As she walked back she noticed that Raoul and Felix were still watching the bench that Catherine, Alice and now Tilly were sitting around. Maybe it was time to get more answers from them?

"How are you doing?" Lola asked as she got to the bench. By the feel of the hairs on the back of her neck, she knew that the Mexicans were loitering behind them. Why were they still watching them? There had to be more to this than they had said, for they were not talking to other owners, but were still obsessed with Catherine's bench. Was it Catherine or Alice they were watching? Lola decided to let her mind mull over this for a while. She would deal with them as soon as she had spoken to her friends. First, she wanted to see if there were any more clues.

"What have you found out?" Tilly asked as she handed Lola a coffee and a muffin.

"Not much." Lola sank into a chair adjusting her position so she could keep an eye on the Mexicans and sipped at the coffee as Sassy tapped her leg. It was amusing, for Raoul was trying to watch them inconspicuously and making a very bad job of it. He peered over a coffee cup and when he caught her eyes he turned so abruptly that he slopped the red hot coffee all over Felix's leg. The other man gasped and batted at his pants, or trousers as they were called in the UK, to try to stop the liquid from burning. More eyes turned to both of them as Lola felt another tap on her leg.

"Hungry!"

Lola took her eyes off Felix patting down his leg and looked down into a pair of begging amber eyes, so she broke off a bit of the muffin and passed it down.

"I thought the police had arrested Maria?" Catherine said. "Isn't this all over?" Catherine's eyes were eager, it was obvious how deeply she felt about this and how much she wanted the case solved.

"The police think so."

"Good, I wanted Una to have justice, but I can't cope with all this stress, we should move on, now that the killer has been caught."

"I don't think it was Maria," Lola said. "If she had done this, then Una would have died before the competition or she would just have been ill. Maria knows her poisons too well."

"It must have been her, and don't be silly, she was poisoned after the competition, they were all jealous of me. They have always been jealous of me," Catherine snapped and folded her arms across her chest in a defensive manner.

"That's intriguing. Do you think she was poisoned before the competition?" Alice asked. She was still looking a little tired and pasty. The shock of her friend's death was taking its toll but her innate curiosity and sense of justice would not let her leave this be.

"I do, she was ill before the competition. Gunter had to go and buy her a coffee because she couldn't face her favorite blackcurrant drink."

"That is unusual," Alice said.

"It proves nothing," Catherine added shaking her head.

"Apparently, she doesn't normally drink coffee before judging," Lola said. "It can make her feel wired, but she was feeling strange and tired so she thought it might help." Lola was watching her friends to see how they took the news. Their reaction was one of mainly shock.

"No, I've never known her to drink coffee before judging," Alice said. "She rarely drank it at all, usually only when there was nothing else available. This is a big clue. I think you are right, she was poisoned before the show."

Catherine harrumphed. "You can't know that, no one can know that!"

"I'm sure the forensic evidence will prove what time she ingested the poison." Lola didn't know this, but she thought it was important. Maybe they could tell, but she had no idea how.

"So, if she was only poorly before the show... are we looking for someone who didn't know what they were doing?" Tilly asked.

"I think so. Who knows, maybe, they didn't even want her dead. Maybe they just wanted to make her too ill to judge?" Lola added as a thought formed in her mind. *Could this be it?*

"Well, I don't know about that." Catherine said. "Surely, the killer acted after the competition because they were angry that I won!"

This was making more and more sense to Lola. "I don't think so; as I said, Una was ill before the judging. That can't have been a coincidence." Lola took another sip of coffee and feeling a tap on her leg she automatically passed a bit of muffin down to Sassy.

Lola had a lot on her mind and she knew that the answers were in there somewhere. However, at the moment, she just couldn't put it all together. What was she missing?

SNIFFIES NIGHT NIGHT

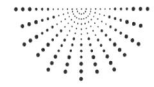

"So what do we do now?" Tilly asked. "Do you have any more ideas on who this could be?"

Lola didn't want to admit that she was struggling. Maybe she should talk to the Mexicans once more, but looking up, she noticed that they had gone. Oh, well, she guessed she had missed out on that one, for now. Maybe she should go for a walk, talk to Sassy and just clear her head.

"How are you all doing?" Lola asked the question, she could see that Sassy was sniffing the air and searching around the bench.

"We're fine," Alice said and Catherine reached out to stroke Sassy just as Raoul and Felix arrived next to the bench.

"Can we talk?" Raoul asked.

"Sniffies night night," Sassy said.

Oh, my goodness, was it the Mexicans after all this? "Where?" Lola asked Sassy.

"Wherever," Raoul said.

"No clear, on air, but been here recently." Sassy sat in front of Lola looking worried that she couldn't be more precise. Lola passed her a bit of muffin and stroked her head in appreciation.

"What do you want?" Catherine asked, her voice harsh and aggressive.

"We have heard rumors and want to talk to detective lady," Raoul said. He turned to Lola once more. "Can we talk?"

Lola's heart was pounding, if Sassy could smell the poison just as they got here it had to be them. But how did she prove it? She could hardly ask them to turn out their pockets! "Of course, Sassy needs to go outside and I could do with some air, do you want to follow me?"

"We will," Felix said and Lola thought he was looking at Queenie.

"Not need to go out," Sassy said, dropping her butt to the ground and sticking out her bottom lip. "Need to search for night night and get bad men who hurt Alice."

Lola was so proud of the little dog and how she wanted to help her friend. She bent down and picked her up. "Maybe sniff out night night on men?" she whispered into the Frenchie's ear.

"Oh, get it now. We need code, so I know you being a trickster."

Lola put Sassy down, her mind-boggling. How would she ever explain that one to her friends? Yeah, I have a secret code for when I want to go talk to my dog in private and am pretending I'm taking her out for a wee! Yep, that was definitely talk that could lead to a trip to crazy town.

"I don't think that's a good idea," Catherine said.

Lola's mind was still on the secret code and pretending that Sassy needed a walk. "Why ever not?"

"They could be... well, look at them... they are drug dealers!" Catherine said.

"Why do people always think we are drug dealers," Felix said, the look in his eyes was of disappointment rather than offense. It was as if he was so used to this, and that it just depressed him.

What did Lola think of that? She too had assumed that the reason Una was worried about the deals was because of something like drugs. She had immediately thought the men were up to no good, and yet, Sassy had smelt no drugs on them. Was this her own prejudice? She hoped not, and blamed it on the fear that Una had shown. Something about the deals had obviously upset Una and Lola's mind had instantly gone to drugs, but it had been wrong. She should have investigated before she jumped to conclusions. After all, she had worried the same about the Sheik, and his motives had been good.

"I apologize," Lola said. "Come, walk with me."

"They could be the killers," Catherine said. "You shouldn't talk to them."

"We are not killers, we wanted to work with Una, why would we kill her?"

Catherine harrumphed again. "I don't like it, just let all this go... the police have the killer."

"Do not worry, there are plenty of people around," Lola said and she pointed toward to door and followed the two men as they walked toward it.

"I should go with them," Lola heard Catherine say.

"No, stay here," Alice said. "Lola can take care of herself."

"Miss Ramsay."

Lola turned to see the smiling face of PC Cronk as he walked towards her. "Just give me a moment," she said to Raoul and Felix and walked over to him.

"Hi," he said, "I just thought you would like to know that we let Maria Ricci go."

"Really, why?"

"She has a very good solicitor; apparently, he is her boyfriend and he, well, if you forgive my French, he tore my boss a new one." The PC was grinning. "This has been such an interesting case, I'm learning a lot."

"Thank you… for letting me know."

"Oh, you were right as well, it was poison." Cronk gave her a conspirator's grin.

"Does Turner have any new suspects?"

"No, how about you?" Cronk asked.

"I might have. I tell you what, if I work out who the killer is I will let you know. Give me your cell number."

"My what?" His face fell and a worried look clouded his eyes. "I live with my mum, not in a cell!"

Lola chuckled. "Your mobile phone number."

Cronk laughed. "Oh, yeah, I was just joshing, I watch lots of CSI."

The more Lola thought about it, the more she was convinced that she knew who the killer was. How to prove it was another matter. Though she knew she had to try, it wasn't going to make her feel any better. Of all the people it could have been, this one was the worst.

Before she could think about it further, Gunter rushed up to her.

"I worked it out," he said.

WORKED IT OUT

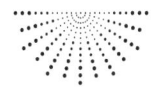

"You worked out who the killer is?" Lola asked, feeling a little stunned and a touch stupid for taking so long.

"What? No, I worked out who the progeny is, or at least I think so." Gunter was holding Una's journal. "Here, look at this."

He was pointing at a line in the journal:

HGQ progeny, R wants back.

Below it Una had written:

I'm not sure about this but it would be a fabulous mating. This could make the breed so much better. How could I achieve this and keep everyone happy? How! How? How!

"I don't know who R is," Gunter said but I know who HGQ is." He was smiling and seemed more alive than he had earlier. Hopefully, solving the murder would give him some comfort.

"R is Raoul Henriquez." Lola pointed over to the two Mexican men, "and that is his partner, Felix Clavel."

"Henvel," Gunter said. "Did they kill my Una?" His fists were clenched by his side and his jaw was clamped tight, as he fought to control his anger.

"It was not them. I think I know who it was, but I'm not sure how to prove it."

Gunter let out a breath. "I help if I can."

"Thank you."

Gunter pointed at the journal once more. "You know who HGQ is?"

"I think that it is Henvel something Queenie," Lola said.

"Not quite, it is Henvel Golden Queen, but you are close enough. Ah," his eyes were wide and his mouth dropped open, "it could not be!" Gunter was shaking his head and red crept into his cheeks.

"Do not do anything, Gunter," Lola said as she watched the man's knuckles whiten where he held the journal.

"I will not, but are you sure?" There was both fury and disappointment in his eyes and they were moist with unshed tears.

"I'm not 100% sure, I think it is. The problem is, I don't know how to prove it." Lola shrugged, but out of the corner of her eye she could see that Raoul was wanting to talk to her, did he have any information? Could she leave Gunter alone now he knew who the killer was?

"I... I... don't know what to do," Gunter said and his hands relaxed.

"Don't do anything, for now, let me find out for certain. I promise I will do that."

"I have to go for a walk, my temper is boiling. Come to me if you need anything or if you can prove it. If not we go to police together," Gunter said.

Lola reached out and squeezed his shoulder. "Don't worry, I will find a way to prove this."

Lola watched him go and when she was sure he was going outside, she crossed back to Raoul and Felix but as she did she whispered down to Sassy. "Can you sniffy night night on the two men?"

"No, it not on them, it on air near Alice." Sassy's eyes were big and sad.

Lola knew that she didn't think that Alice was the killer, that she had just used her name because she was on her mind. The little Frenchie was worried for her friend, and so was Lola. If the killer turned out to be who she thought it was, then Alice was in for another shock.

WHERE IS THE POISON

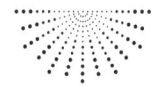

"I'm sorry about that," Lola said to Raoul and Felix. "What did you want to speak to me about?"

The two men looked at each other and Felix nodded, indicating for Raoul to do the talking.

"We are not bad men," Raoul said. "We not watching you because we are killers." His hands floated up into the air and he clenched his fists in front of him in frustration. "We just want to breed dogs. Our Henvel line is doing so well that we just wanted the most famous dog we ever bred to come back, just for a little while. For photos and such. Is that so wrong?"

"No, it's not wrong but you should not have blackmailed Una to give the prize to Queenie."

Raoul's eyes widened and he shook his head.

"No, no, we did not do this," Felix said. "We never expected Henvel Golden Queen to even win her group at such a prestigious show as this. We were just, how you say, jumping the moon, because she was a champion and had qualified to get here."

"Over the moon," Raoul said. "And Felix is right, we were so happy that Queenie was here at all, nothing else mattered." He shook his head again. "I... we never tried to bribe Una, but I doubt we could have. She was a clever and principled lady. She helped us choose the dogs we have now and she helped us breed this litter." His hand waved in the general direction of Queenie. "We wanted Una to come and judge at our show and help us choose the best dogs to breed from. We were so excited about it. We wanted Queenie to come too..."

"I understand, but Catherine didn't want to let you have Queenie, did she?" Lola asked.

"We didn't explain it well enough to her," Raoul said. "At first, we wanted to buy her and to keep her. Una was not happy, we had made this part of the contract and

Una was so upset, but we did not understand. Una explained it all to us, and so we made a proposal to her today. One that all would be happy with."

Lola waited for him to explain but it seemed that he thought he had already done so. "What was the proposal?" she finally asked.

"Oh, pardon. We were to borrow Queenie and Catherine could have come with her." Raoul shrugged. "Yet now, we are thought of as either drug dealers or murderers."

"Maybe drug dealing murderers!" Felix added.

"I don't think you are either of those," Lola said. "What did Catherine think of this new offer?"

"She would not speak to us," Raoul said. "We agreed on it with Una this morning, but Una was not feeling well. Catherine was talking to her before we went in and we tried to speak to Catherine after... but she wouldn't talk to us, still won't... maybe you can put in a good word for us?"

"Maybe," Lola said. "Leave this with me. Don't try to talk to Catherine again... Go and wait for me at the place where they sell cream teas." Lola pointed to the side of the arena where she had seen the place that sold cream teas and served tea in China cups. It was easy to spot and would keep the two men out of the way for now. What was it called? "The Cottage Tea Room."

"Okay, we see you soon?" Raoul asked.

"It won't be instantly, but I will come to you. I have to prove who killed Una first."

"Do you know?" Felix asked.

"Yes, I do."

As Lola watched the men walk away, she wondered what the killer could have done with the bottle of poison. She could have hidden it on one of the benches or put it in a trash can, or a bin, as it was called here in the UK. There were plenty of them dotted around the building. Maybe, if they found it, there would be fingerprints or DNA evidence on the bottle. It was a long shot, but it was a start.

"Hey, Sassy," Lola said and the Frenchie looked up at her with her big amber eyes and her little tail wagging. Sassy was eager to help. "I want you to search all around this area for night night, can you do that?"

"You mean sniffies for it?" Sassy asked.

"I do."

Sassy gave a woof of affirmation and began to search along the benches. She was taking great big sniffs, really loud sniffs, and looked a little odd. A few of the competitors gave her strange looks but then soon went back to their own lives. Sassy searched around the benches and in people's bags. Luckily, she was small and most people gave her a quick glance and closed their bags but soon forgot her.

"Oh!" Sassy ran forward and gobbled down a treat that was on the floor. She looked up to see Lola watching her and grinned. "Sorry, but it was there!"

"Keep searching, Sweetie," Lola said.

"I always search for sweeties," Sassy said.

"No, that was not what I meant." Lola tried not to chuckle.

Sassy sat down in her confused pose. "Not want me to search?"

"Yes, I do, but for night night, not sweeties." Lola shrugged.

"You strange," Sassy said. "You say do it, then change mind. Can't help if sweeties find their way into my mouth. If they there, and I accidentally eat them, it not my fault."

"I believe you," Lola said and of course, Sassy was pleased with this answer. With a little skip of joy, she went back to her sniffing. Lola had to learn that few things could overrule the Frenchie's stomach.

"Not here," Sassy said again and again as she searched the benches and bins. Only punctuated with the occasional "Oh, mine." Along with little nom-nom sounds as she munched down a discarded treat.

They had finished one side and as they crossed to the other side of the benches Sassy stopped and sniffed the air. "Here," she said.

It looked like they had found the poison."

YOU GOT IT?

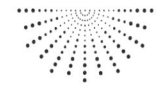

"You got it?" Lola asked.

Sassy sank to the floor, sticking out her back legs and pouting. "Sorry, lost it."

Lola felt a rush of disappointment but she would not let Sassy know, Sassy was already feeling as if she had let her down and needed a boost. "You are doing great," Lola said. "Where did you sniffy it?"

The problem was Sassy could smell or sense emotions and she looked a little down for a moment. Lola smiled even wider and Sassy couldn't resist, her eyes brightened.

"On air, all around here," Sassy said, "but sniffies weak, I lost it. Lots of other delicious sniffies, maybe I too hungry to tell?" She peered at Lola making her eyes as wide and sad as she could, and she seemed to shrug.

"Maybe," Lola said and she handed down a tiny fish treat that she kept in her pocket. They were small and shaped like a fish, they smelled delicious, well, to Sassy. It seemed to do the trick.

Sassy was on the move again, she searched in a big circle all around where she had found the scent, but she was unable to pick it up again. Lola could understand why. There was a burger stall just down from there and a lot of people were eating.

Gently, Lola guided her along the opposite side of the benches where she once again began sniffies through all of the bags, crates, benches, and paraphernalia that were there.

"Not here," she said and moved along. "Not, here, oh." The tug on the lead grew stronger and Lola tried to say something, but it was too late. Sassy had gobbled down a bit of dog treat. "Um, delicious, me able to sniffy better already."

Sassy had her head down and her little tail was waving in the air as she sniffed and snorted along the benches.

"How could you?"

Lola heard a woman's voice shout, the accent was clear, it was Maria."

"I'm sorry, I know I was wrong but… I'm sorry." Mark was holding out Maria's missing lead and was minus his jacket. The lead sparkled under the lights and Phillip looked proud standing behind him.

Maria snatched the diamond-encrusted luck off him and held it to her chest. "We would have won." She checked the lead over and then placed it behind her in a bag that she then zipped up and moved to stand in front of. Glaring, she pointed a finger at Mark tapping it against his chest. "You are a cheat, a dirty, rotten, cheat!"

"Take that back," Mark said, his cheeks were red and his fists were clenched at his side.

"Keep doing sniffies, but don't go far from me," Lola said as she wandered a little closer to the kerfuffle.

"Will not!" Maria shrieked and she beat her hands against Mark's hot pink chest. "You evil man, I bet you killed her in anger!"

Mark stepped back, his face so red it almost matched his shirt. "I told you to take that back!" Mark stepped closer and peered down at the angry, aristocratic woman. The rage on his face was clear and he was clenching his fist at his sides.

A lilac blur appeared between the two of them and Sassy let out a Frenchie scream. Both of them stepped back, shock opening their eyes to such an extent that Lola wondered if they would pop out of their heads.

"That's enough," Lola said. She turned to Maria. "I know he did wrong, but he could have just hidden the lead, *your luck*, and said nothing. That would have been the easier option. He apologized and you should accept it."

She turned to Mark. Phillip was standing behind him, his hands fluttering out towards Mark. It appeared he was torn between comforting his partner and the fear of the situation. "Enough is enough, you have said your piece, now go."

Mark looked a little sheepish and nodded, but before he could go, Maria was striking out at him again. She almost knocked Sassy flying as she launched an attack on the man's hot pink-shirted chest.

"What have we here?" the commanding tones of DI Turner cut through the shrieking. "Cronk, arrest them both."

The noise stopped and Maria stepped back. "It is nothing," she said. "I apologize, Mark forgive me. I was just angry."

Cronk froze with a set of handcuffs held before him.

Mark was standing tall, his bottom lip stuck out almost as much as Sassy's could and he was refusing to look at her. Phillip tapped him on the back and cleared his throat.

"Oh, all right," Mark said and he turned to Cronk. "It was nothing, just a disagreement and I accept Maria's apology." Mark turned to walk away but was stopped by Turner stepping in front of him.

"Not so fast." Turner turned to Cronk. "I said arrest them, I'm sure one of them is involved. We will sort it all out at the station."

Lola watched as the two made arrangements for their dogs and were then taken away. PC Cronk offered her an apologetic smile.

Once they were gone, Lola felt exhausted. The police had taken away the wrong people, but she was still no closer to proving it.

Sassy began to search again and made her way down the benches. Though she sniffed and snorted and tried her hardest, she couldn't reacquire the scent. Lola was beginning to think that it was a lost cause. Was there another way that she could prove who did this? There had to be, but even as she racked her brain she couldn't work it out.

A tap on her leg had her glancing down. Sassy was staring up at her with a smile on her face. "I help," she said.

"I don't know how you can." Lola smiled and bent down to stroke the little Frenchie.

"You should have a treat, that always helps me." Sassy's little tongue flicked out from her lips and back in again. It was clear that she could manage another treat. Lola couldn't understand where she put it all but the dog was in perfect condition. Lola handed her a fish treat.

"These scrummy," Sassy said. "Why you not eat them?"

Lola chuckled, as much as her little four-legged friend liked the treats, they didn't appeal to Lola. They were hard and dry and very fishy. "I don't like them."

"No, you telling fibbies." Sassy's eyes were wide and then her mouth dropped open and she moved over to rub her face under Lola's hand. "I understand, you do for me, save all treats so I can have them. I lovey loves you so much."

Lola picked her up and kissed her head. "I'd do anything for you."

"Me do anything for you too, when you stuck, you need a friend."

As Lola stood up she had an idea. It might not solve the murder, but maybe it would help. And yet, why was it this friend that came to mind?

PHONE A FRIEND

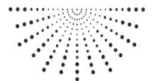

*L*ola pulled out her phone and wandered outside the building once more. As they left, she showed her pass to the security guard, and then she walked Sassy over to the grass. As was always the case, the little dog soon found herself sniffing.

Once she was finished, Lola took them over to a bench and sat down, Sassy jumped up and sat on her knee. Leaning back against her. "I have idea," Sassy said. "We have cake, then do more sniffies! Both great fun, make us feel better."

"More cake!"

"Well, or donut, or milky think, or pizzle, or I saw other nice things... you choose."

"I don't think that will help. I'm going to talk to a friend." Lola rubbed Sassy's head before she scrolled through her phone. For some reason, she wanted to talk to Linc. It was strange for her, but she wondered if he could give her any advice. Or did she just want to speak to him?

It didn't matter, she dialed the number and waited.

"Hello, Lola, it's good to hear from you," Linc said.

For the first time in a while, Lola heard the song going through her mind. The one with her name in. Though Linc had never teased her, as many others had, for some reason the almost sing-song tone of his voice brought back bad memories. For a moment, she almost hung up. Instead, she swallowed down her worries. She had been told that dating again may bring back bad memories and that if it did her mind would try to push her away from the man in question. Maybe this was just that!

"Hi, I just wanted to run something past you, get another set of ideas... if that's all right?"

"That's great, I'll be any help I can, fire away."

"Sorry, Linc, it's good to hear your voice, were you in the middle of anything?"

He chuckled. "No, I was... promise you won't laugh?"

"I promise," she said, feeling a little worried as well as a little intrigued.

"I was just reading up about... well, about ghosts..."

"I wasn't expecting that," Lola said and wasn't sure if to laugh or not.

"I have a friend who thinks he keeps seeing them," Linc said. "I guess, well, when you've seen some of the things I... and I'm sure you have... it is hard to believe in ghosts and also hard not to. Sorry, I'm rambling, is there something I can do for you?"

Lola understood what he meant, or at least she thought she did. The horrors of war still haunted her and it would be nice to believe in a way to come back. Sometimes, what they had been through made people lose their faith, but it had only strengthened hers. "It sounds intriguing," she said before she even realized that she was doing so. "Maybe I can help you out with your friend. I once looked into a fake psychic." Lola remembered the case she called Seeing Through the Séance. Sassy had been a big help in proving that the woman was a cheat and a thief.

"That would be great, now, what can I help you with?"

Lola felt herself let out a breath and some tension with it, there was something about Linc's voice that relaxed her. Quickly, she explained what was going on and that she needed to prove who the killer was.

"You do live an exciting life," he said. "Do you think finding the bottle of poison would help?"

"I do, I guess it's all I've got... well, I haven't got it... have I?"

Linc chuckled. "Why don't you let the killer hear you saying that the police think they know where the bottle is and that they are going for it shortly and will be checking it for DNA or fingerprints, or whatever CSI type of thingy they can. Hopefully, this will flush the killer out. They will try to get the bottle before the police do."

"Thank you," Lola said and she almost hung up the phone. Her counselor had told her that she got too involved in her own life. That there were times when she got excited and forgot about other people and their feelings. "That is really helpful... what are you planning for the rest of the day?"

Linc chuckled. "You don't have to humor me. I can tell that you are chomping at the bit to go and find the killer.

Go for it, and let me know what happens later. It was really nice to be useful."

"You were a big help, sometimes, I just need to bounce ideas off someone else."

"I thought you have Alice, Tilly, and Tanya for that," he said.

"Tanya's not here today, a dog show is not really her cup of tea." Lola couldn't believe she was already starting to use such a British phrase and she almost chuckled. "I didn't want to upset Alice and Tilly. They are taking this hard."

"I understand. Go, set this up, but know that I am rooting for you and that I am here if you need an extra ear."

"Good to know," Lola said. "Speak to you soon." She hung up the phone but how could she set this up in a way that would work. The killer had to hear her, but also could not imagine that they were under suspicion.

SETTING UP A STING

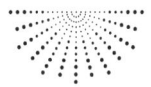

*L*ola knew that she needed a good idea and also a way to film what happened. She remembered seeing a stall earlier. It was one selling action cameras. These were small camera's that you could attach to your pet, the film quality had been remarkable. Maybe that would help?

Lola knew that it would be hard to prove, the hall was buzzing with people, and once the trap was set the killer could go off in 4 main directions. It would be difficult for Lola to keep an eye on all of them, she needed help.

They went back into the exhibition center and were amazed that it was still so crowded. People were milling everywhere, there were so many of them that it would be easy for someone to get lost in the crowd. If she lost them, then this would all be for nothing, she had no evidence. If she let that happen then Una's killer would go free, or even worse, the wrong person would be punished. Lola felt a buzz of excitement, she had to make this work.

Weaving through the crowd, and as she made her way back to the bench, she remembered Raoul and Felix. That would work, she also spotted PC Cronk bagging up items from Mark Duncan's bench. Phillip was there looking after the dogs and looking most despondent.

Lola approached Phillip first. "How are you doing?" she asked and then almost groaned inside at the inane question.

Sassy knew what to do, she was leaning against Phillip's leg. He picked her up and cuddled her close as he fought the tears in his eyes. "I wanted to go with him, but I have to wait for a friend to come and take the dogs. It is awful, what can I do? I know he didn't do this."

Sassy whined in his arms and licked his face.

"Oh, look at you, trying to cheer silly old Phillip up," he said.

"She's much better at it than me, but I may be able to help." Lola noticed a spark of hope in his eyes. "I think I can prove who did this. If I do, we will get Mark out. Even if I don't I will help him."

"Bless you." Phillip hugged her and she could feel Sassy lick her cheek as she became a sandwich in the hug. "I know you are an angel," Phillip said. "Is there anything I can do to help?"

Lola explained what she was going to do and asked if the person came this way if he could follow them and call Lola so she could be there when they found the bottle.

"That is easy, I am ready." Phillip was looking much stronger.

Lola left him and went across to PC Cronk. She explained the same to him and told him what she intended to do. He agreed to help, albeit a little reluctantly.

"What if Turner finds out?" he asked.

"He will… when you give him the real killer!"

Cronk's miserable face broke into a big smile.

Next, Lola made her way to the stand selling proper tea in proper cups and saw the two men sharing an elaborate cream tea. Sassy rushed over and scratched at Raoul's leg as she sat before him her eyes all eager.

Raoul laughed. "Are you hungry, little dog?"

"Am yes, me," Sassy woofed.

Raoul looked at Lola, she nodded and he handed down a bit of scone with cream and jam.

Sassy savored the treat, licking her lips to make sure she got every sticky morsel.

Lola took a seat and explained her plan. She wanted the two men to go to some of the benches enquiring if any dogs were for sale and then to let it slip that the police knew where the poison was. Lola had decided to say that they had special equipment that could track it down, they were waiting on a warrant before they collected it. They also had to say that the police didn't know they had been overheard.

Raoul and Felix were eager to help. "I think we should go straight away," Felix said.

"Yes, do, but let me know before you get to the final bench, I want to have everyone in place," Lola said.

"We will." Raoul looked proud and eager to be part of the investigation.

Sassy looked at the platter of cakes and let out a little whine. Lola heard, "Can't leave all those cakes, give to me."

"Once you have done that, if you go to the side entrance of the main ring, if our killer goes past you, let me know and follow discreetly. You have a cell... mobile, you can take pictures or videos of what happens if I don't get there. We need proof of them getting the poison bottle."

"We can do this, it will take a while. Please," Raoul pointed to the table. "Enjoy a cake or two."

Lola sat down, she had eaten enough cake for one day, maybe a whole month, but she knew someone who wouldn't mind sharing all of it. However, she broke off the tiniest of pieces to hand down to Sassy. After all, the little bulldog had been very busy today.

Now they had to get their own equipment to make sure that the sting was well and truly set up.

DRAMA QUEEN

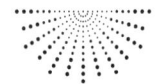

Raoul and Felix began to wander along the benches. The idea was that they would convince people that they were looking for different dogs. They wanted the killer to let their guard down, they wanted Catherine to feel as if Queenie was no longer of interest to them.

They spent time looking at Gunter's GSD, Thor. Gunter was still not there and another man, very similar in build to Gunter was watching the dog. "Is there something you want?" he asked in a clipped tone.

"We are just looking at different breeds," Raoul said. "We are wanting to start new kennels."

"I understand and Thor is a magnificent specimen of his breed. Unfortunately, I'm just a friend of Gunter's, he would be able to give you more information but he is... unavailable at the moment. I can give you his card." The man handed over a card with a picture of Thor on it.

Raoul nodded his thanks and then wandered further along the benches. At times they stopped to talk to people and said they were looking to purchase dogs and then they would let slip their snippet of information. Most people were shocked and they hoped that the killer would be caught soon, others looked at the two men as if they had no right to get involved.

Felix tapped Raoul's shoulder. "Don't look but we are being watched."

"Hopefully, it is working," Raoul said. "I would like to punish this killer."

"Do you think it would help us?" Felix asked.

Raoul shook his head, his brown eyes narrowing. "We must not think of this in selfish ways. We are doing what is right."

Felix averted his gaze and rubbed at his nose, a sign he was feeling a little guilty, but he nodded his agreement. "We should carry on."

"Yes." Raoul swallowed, it was very crowded at the moment and he longed to be back in Mexico, walking on the beach with his dogs.

* * *

Lola made her way to the stall that was selling cameras.

"Are you interested?" a young woman with purple hair asked, and though she smiled, it didn't seem genuine.

"I am." Lola smiled and hoped that she could get something to work.

"What is it for, sports? Not with this little one, I imagine." The woman's looks held a touch of disdain as her eyes flicked over Sassy.

Sassy barked, bouncing on all four legs with each bark. That took her closer to her distractor and the woman backed away.

"I'll give you small," Sassy growled.

"You would be surprised," Lola said, handing a treat down to Sassy. It worked, her little friend sat next to her and leaned against her leg, making nom-nom sounds. Lola could hardly tell the sales assistant that she wanted the Frenchie to follow a killer, and for a moment her mind was blank.

"Well, these cameras strap to any harness. I need to know the size of dog it will be used on and the quality you need before I can recommend something." The woman's tone was getting a touch snotty now and she glanced around to see if there was a better prospect.

"Apologies," Lola said. "It is for Sassy here and I need..." Quality that will hold up in court would only bring questions. "Good enough quality to see people's faces."

"I see, we have plenty of those but they are expensive."

Lola nodded her acceptance. Her PI business was doing well and this camera could come in handy on other cases too. A voice in her head told her that she had plenty of money, but for some reason that always made her feel guilty.

The frosty woman's face turned into a genuine smile. "Let me show you."

Within a few more minutes Lola was walking away with the camera strapped to Sassy and an app on her phone. This should work.

"Feels funny," Sassy said. "I need to roll, need to scratch my back."

"No!" Lola almost yelled and Sassy sat up looking at her with wide eyes.

"Drama Queen!" Sassy said.

"It was expensive and that might break it."

"Money silly," Sassy said.

"Money pays for treats and food to fill Frenchie's tummies, money is needed for squeaky leggy things!" Lola raised her eyebrows.

"I not scratch it off. I get treat?" Sassy's eyes were wide with hope.

"Maybe," Lola said. "Come on, we have a killer to catch."

As they walked away she received a text from Raoul saying he was going to talk to Peter. Lola knew that the plan would soon be in place and she needed to get her ducks in a row.

Quickly, she sent a text to Tilly, asking her to meet her and another to PC Cronk and Phillip saying they were ready. Now all she had to do was hope things would go well.

Tilly turned up with a smile on her face, but Lola got the impression that it was forced. "How are you doing?" she asked.

"I'm okay, I just want to help Alice. You said the police arrested Maria and Mark, have they got the right person?"

"I don't think so and that is what I wanted to talk to you about." Lola quickly explained her thoughts and the plan. "I'm pretty sure it will be my direction that she travels, that was where Sassy got the scent, but just in case."

Tilly looked 10 years older and tired but she put a smile on her face. "I understand, I will watch if the killer goes around the right side of the arena. I will let you know." Tilly rubbed Lola's arm. "This is not your fault, don't take it so hard.

"I'm worried about Alice."

"She is strong and justice is what will help her heal."

Tilly pulled Lola into a hug before making her way back to Alice. It felt good to be in her arms, secure and safe. Lola was so grateful for her good friends and she hated to hurt them, even when it was the right... the only thing she could do.

With Tilly gone she had one area covered, Lola and Sassy would cover the area where Sassy had found and then lost the scent. This was all coming together.

* * *

Raoul and Felix were looking at Big Bruce. The boxer had been fast asleep on his bench but when he noticed the men approach he sat up so proud and regal.

"We would like to know more about the breed," Felix said.

"Oh, boxers are just marvelous," Peter was smiling so brightly that his face might crack. "Fun, loyal, brave dogs that can do whatever it is they are asked."

Raoul knew that his face gave him away. He had heard that they were silly dogs that farted and drooled a lot. Surely, this man was just embellishing the facts! "Would they make good guard dogs?" Raoul asked.

"Of course, they are the best... well, in my opinion," Peter shrugged and smiled. "They are said to be the gentle guard dogs, as they body slam, rather than use teeth, in the first instance. They are very vigilant. When they bark, it usually means something. People see the goofy doofus and think they can't do anything but they were one of the first breeds to be used as police dogs, they have been guide dogs for the blind, search and rescue dogs, dogs used in war, they have done every dog sport and still can, if their fun loving character is encouraged in the right direction."

"This is impressive," Raoul said.

"I thought they just drooled a lot and sat on the sofa," Felix added.

Peter chuckled. "They can do that also. They can be very relaxed dogs but it is said that they know when there is danger, and will always react to save their owner." Peter shook his head. "I am lucky, I have never needed to test this, but I'm sure Bruce would protect me with his life."

Bruce gave a big deep woof that seemed to confirm this.

"We are very interested," Raoul said and reached forward to stroke Bruce. The big dog leaned into the contact and closed his eyes to enjoy it.

"He's enjoying that, and I have one of his puppies that will be available in 5 weeks. I would need to know more about you before I agreed to let you have him," Peter said.

"I understand. You can search our website. www.HenvelPerrosdeCaza.com."

"I will do that," Peter said.

"Just before we go, have you heard that the police have found the poison?" Felix asked.

"Well, they think they know where it is," Raoul added.

Peter's eyes blinked rapidly and his mouth opened, but for a moment nothing came out. "How! And who is the killer?"

"They have this equipment that can trace scents in the air." Raoul shrugged. "It sounded very technical. I was just behind them, they didn't even know I was there and it was fascinating."

"You said they think they know where it is?" Peter asked. "Haven't they got it yet?"

"Ah," Felix waved a finger in the air. "They have to get a warrant. In our country, they would get the evidence first, not risk losing it."

"Well, that would depend on if bribes were being made," Raoul said.

"Not all our police are like that," Felix said.

"I guess, things are changing." Raoul shrugged.

"We have to look at other dogs, but we like what we see," Felix said and the two men made their way to the next bench. They were getting better at this and they knew that they had been watched. Now, they hoped that they would be able to put the plan into operation and help catch the killer.

THE FAMOUS QUEENIE

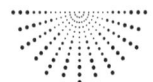

*L*ola and Sassy were in position, she had watched Raoul and Felix leave Peter's bench and make their way over to Catherine's. Now it was all to play for, would she talk to them or would she still refuse? If she turned them away then Lola had another idea, she could get Tilly to do the same thing. She didn't want to, though.

It was a lot to ask and she didn't want to put that pressure on her friend.

"You sad again," Sassy said as she pawed at Lola's leg.

"I just wish people wouldn't be bad and kill each other," Lola said.

Sassy looked confused. "Bad is bad, is silly to expect bad people to be anything other than bad. Like cake is cake and you wouldn't expect it to be… fish. Still, I like both… or all. I could eat cake… if there is any… or fish."

Lola chuckled and picked Sassy up. "You have a way of cheering me up."

Sassy snuggled against Lola's cheek. "I like you to be happy, happy best, sad silly. Cake makes me happy."

"Later," Lola said and put the Frenchie down. Right now, she needed to concentrate on the task at hand. A lot was riding on this and they had to get it right.

Raoul's palms were sweaty as he and Felix made their way to Catherine's bench. The pressure was mounting. He wanted to catch the killer for Una's sake. He had liked and respected her, but it was also a way for him to show that he was a good man and not the drug-dealing killer that many expected him to be.

The benches area was crowded once more, a lot of people were milling about and he found it a little claustrophobic. As he was bumped by a large man, who was not looking, and didn't even stop, he felt panic clawing up inside of him. The urge to flee was overwhelming but a hand touched his back.

"We are doing good," Felix said. "We'll soon get this done and find a good dog to take back."

"I hope we can do that, but I doubt it will be today. Hopefully, Lola will be able to find people for us to talk to."

"She will," Felix said. "We might not get Queenie, but our dreams are not over."

Raoul nodded, the crowd had thinned a bit and he felt better. "What do you think about Bruce?"

"I liked him, I could see us with dogs like that, maybe as another project."

Raoul smiled. "I agree, my wife would like him, and my daughters too. Now, let's do something good, first."

Felix slapped him on the back.

Raoul and Felix made their way through the crowds to Catherine's bench, it was not far but took them a few minutes as a group of people had congregated on the benches in between Peter and Catherine. Raoul was trying not to stare, but he knew that Catherine was watching them all the time.

"Congratulations," he said when they arrived in front of her.

Catherine was standing next to Queenie, her hand on the dog's neck, her face stern, and her eyes narrowed. It looked like she was still very wary of them. Between her and Raoul were Tilly and Alice. Alice's expression mirrored that of Catherine's, her chin was raised in defiance, and there was no hint of a smile on her face. Tilly's appearance was softer and she gave Raoul and Felix a quick smile of encouragement.

"Why are you here?" Catherine snapped. "I already told you, you will not steal my Queenie."

"Apologies," Felix said. "That was never our intention. We only wished to have her come as a... celebrity... famous... how you say?" He looked at Raoul.

"We just wanted Queenie to come over and have some pictures taken at our kennels. She is the most famous dog to have come out of our state and we brought her into this world. We are so proud to be known for the famous Queenie. We would have loved to mate her to our dog... but mainly just wanted her to visit, and you could have come too. We would look after you, it would have been like a holiday; our place is nice with a swimming pool and beach... it is very safe." His head dropped for he needed to hide the look in his eyes. It was meant to be sorrow and conciliation, but anger was creeping in there and he didn't want Catherine to see it. "It is not to be now, we understand," he said raising his eyes.

The color had drained from Catherine's face and she stumbled back and clung onto the bench. It was as if she had almost fainted and needed the support to stay upright.

"Are you all right?" Alice asked and she turned an angry gaze on Raoul. "I can chase these leeches away if you wish." Alice was almost snarling.

"No, it is all right." Catherine seemed to have recovered, though she was still pale she had let go of the bench. As they watched her bottom lip quivered and it was clear that she was fighting back tears.

"We wanted to apologize, if you got the wrong idea, if we upset you," Raoul said. "That was not what we wanted and now... with everything that has happened we would never ask about Queenie at all."

"Really," Catherine said. "I would have been willing to accept such terms. I would just never let Queenie be taken from me... I love her so much... you understand?"

"Of course, we do." Raoul smiled. "Now, we should leave you to celebrate and to speak to all those who want a picture with Queenie. Maybe you would send us a good one?"

"Yes, yes, of course," Catherine said. "Come and speak to me in about an hour. Maybe we can do something more."

"We will." Raoul leaned in closer and looked behind him as if he wanted to check that no one was listening. "I heard the police talking earlier. They didn't know I was listening." Once more he checked behind him and he noticed as he looked back that Catherine's face was eager and that she had moved a little closer. She was almost in his face and he was finding it a little uncomfortable.

"What did they say?" Catherine asked.

"Have they found the killer?" Alice asked as she stuck her head between the two of them.

"The case is closed, they arrested Maria and Mark." Catherine moved back and folded her arms across her chest, but she leaned in once more eager to hear the news.

"Well," Raoul said and paused, wanting to create some suspense. He could see that Catherine was desperate to get him to talk. So much so that he thought she might shake him if he didn't hurry up. "They said that they had detected the poison." Raoul pointed over to the area where Sassy had sniffed it out. "They had traced it back and were going to retrieve it soon."

"Soon," Alice said. "Why not now?"

"They said something about a warrant." Raoul shrugged. "The good news is they are sure there will be DNA on the bottle."

"They shouldn't need...," Alice started and then made a grunt as Tilly kicked her ankle and elbowed her ribs. Alice looked at Tilly and changed her mind. "Yes, that is right. Oh, this is exciting."

"They would never get DNA off the bottle... would they? What about fingerprints?" Catherine's mouth had fallen open.

"They think they can, the type of glass or something," Raoul said. "There was a young policeman asking lots of questions, just like you."

"We should leave you and apologize once more," Felix said and he took Raoul's arm to guide him away.

"Of course, come talk to me," Catherine called after them.

"I don't know why you want to talk to them," Alice said. "I don't like them, I think that they still want to take Queenie."

"Maybe, originally." Catherine smiled and shifted on her feet. It was almost like a young child who needed the toilet. "I could have dealt with them on this proposal, though. Why, didn't they say this to me this morning?"

"Are you all right?" Tilly asked, for Catherine was still going from foot to foot and almost swaying where she stood.

"I need the ladies, can you two keep an eye on Queenie for me?" Without waiting for an answer, Catherine left.

"What was that about?" Alice asked Tilly as they watched Catherine disappear."

"I will tell you later, for now, I have to keep my eye on Catherine."

"Oh, no!" Alice said and she stumbled back to the bench, sat down, and put her arm around Queenie.

SASSYING TO THE EVIDENCE

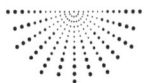

"Why you stressed?" Sassy was tapping Lola's leg and staring up at her with big sorrowful amber eyes.

"I'm not," Lola said as she forced herself to keep still and clenched her hands a little to stop them from fiddling with her cell. This was part of her military training, and usually, she could fool people into thinking that she was fine, even when her heart would be racing and she was terrified that things would go wrong. That was not what was happening here... well, not entirely. Her heart was racing and she was afraid that if this went wrong that the killer would escape.

Of course, she was also worried about the consequences of it going right; Alice would be devastated.

"Are too," Sassy said.

"How can you tell?" Lola asked, glancing down at her dog for a moment before looking back up. The last thing she needed to do was miss Catherine as she went for the poison.

"Heart fast, skin sweaty, sniffies different. You can't tell porkies to me."

"Porkies?" Lola had to ask and she felt a smile on her face. Which of course, relaxed her a little and she managed to shake off the fear. She could do this and what would be, would be. Alice was strong and they would get her through this.

"Porky pies, lies," Sassy said.

"Was that Tony who told you that?" Lola asked.

"Me thinks... but could have been Alice.

Lola had received texts from all the people who were watching, she knew that they were ready and alert. Phillip had let her know that Catherine came past him and he was following. At first, she had thought about going to him but it was in the opposite direction of the scent of poison. Something told her to hold her ground.

She just prayed that this would work. Phillip would film anything that was needed.

"There," Sassy said.

Lola looked to her right and followed the dog's gaze. Catherine was crossing the hall. It looked like she had skirted her way around the hall and was coming back to the benches. Her head was down and she was wearing a different jacket and a floppy brown hat. Lola would have never spotted her until she got closer.

A text notification pinged on her phone.

I lost her, sorry, Phillip.
Don't worry, I have her, Lola replied.

Catherine was being furtive, stopping and glancing around and keeping herself among crowds. It would have worked for a lot of people, but Lola was used to this and Sassy could sniffy her out.

Catherine took one last look around and dived into the ladies' room. "Follow her," Lola said and Sassy set off across the hall. The little Frenchie arrived at the ladies just as the door opened and another lady came out. Sassy snook in and was gone.

Lola felt her heart really kick up now. She had sent her friend into danger and she hated it. The problem was, if Catherine saw her come in, she would leave the poison and they might not find it.

Lola looked at her phone and watched the video that showed a view of the room through Sassy's ears. The camera was mounted on her back. You could just see the tips of her ears on the video as she moved her head. The little dog walked into the cream-tiled bathroom. Four people were standing at the basins, but none of them was Catherine. Sassy sat down under the sink and behind a trash can, or a bin, as the British would call it. She would be hidden here and she looked across at the stalls. All five doors were closed.

Two more people came in and queued up for the stalls. Sassy adjusted so she could see around them, she was so clever.

There was sound on the video and Lola imagined Sassy was desperate to tell her which stall Catherine was in. Lola had spoken to her and told her that she mustn't talk or she might be taken out of there by a good Samaritan. She also warned her not to find the poison herself. They needed proof that Catherine knew where it was.

Sassy was staring at the stall on the very left and also at the trash can closest to it. For a moment, the sound of Sassy sniffing was very loud, then there was a grumble, "Sorry, forgot." Luckily, it was hidden by the sound of running water.

Sassy was still staring at the left stall. That made sense. Sassy's head moved to the right and Lola saw a woman leave the next stall with a little boy in tow. Another woman took her place. Lola could hear the mumbled conversation but ignored it for it was nothing to do with the case. Sassy turned straight back to her prize and stared at the door on the left.

Lola forced herself to breathe and keep her eyes on the video. She wanted to let her people know what was happening but decided to keep her eyes and mind on the bathroom.

Another stall opened, Sassy looked so quickly that Lola felt a little dizzy but she didn't have time to focus on the person before Sassy was back staring at the door. The ambient noise changed as the stall was filled with another person and the sound of the faucet, tap as the British called it, running, was very loud. The woman must be just above Sassy and yet the video was clear. Maybe she was angled so she could see?

It seemed like forever and Lola wondered if Catherine had the poison and was flushing it. Panic made her want to run in there, but she couldn't, her barging in would not help. If that was the case, then she had misjudged this and had to hope to find another way to catch the killer. The bottle, surely that would not flush?

Lola let out a breath to calm herself as the door to the left cubicle cracked open. Surely, Catherine was not going to peek out to see if anyone was there? That would look suspicious.

But she did. Catherine poked her head around the door and then pulled it back and shut it. The restroom was crowded. There was a constant stream of people coming in. Seconds passed and Lola kept still, it was almost as if she was afraid that Catherine would hear if she moved, or even took a breath.

The door opened again, more confidently this time. Catherine came out and crossed to the sinks. Lola gasped.

That was not what she expected and she couldn't see her anymore. All she could imagine was that Catherine was washing her hands. The video was a little shaky, Sassy was finding it hard to sit still.

Catherine crossed the room to the paper towel dispenser and pulled out a few towels. Sassy moved along under the counter so she could see better. Catherine threw the towel in the bin and then her hands went up and she looked at her fingers. She was feigning that she had lost a ring. "Oh, my ring," Lola heard over the video.

Catherine began to root around in the trash can that held all the dirty towels. She was shaking her head and making quite a fuss. Her hair was falling over her face and she batted it away with some annoyance. A hand and arm reached down. Someone was trying to help her.

"Let me help."

Panicked, Catherine pushed the hand away and even in the tiny video, Lola could see the fear on her face. "Leave me, I can do it," Catherine shrieked. The fear on her face changed to apology but the person never came back into view.

Lola clicked over to her text app and sent a text.

I think she has it, get to the ladies' room opposite the benches.

With that done, Lola went back to the video. Catherine put something in her pocket and stood up with a big smile on her face. She was coming, where was Cronk?

Lola wandered across to the entrance of the ladies' room. Catherine came out and almost walked into her.

"Oh, sorry, are you just going in?" Catherine asked.

"No, I was waiting for you."

"Whatever do you mean?" Catherine's eyes were wide, her face drained of blood and she stepped back quickly. "Do I need to call security?"

"That's no problem, Ma'am," PC Cronk said. "Maybe I will do." He winked at Lola and then stepped up to Catherine.

Lola felt a tap on her leg and looked down to see Sassy. "Did I do good?"

"You certainly did," Lola said and passed down a fishy treat.

"Certainly did what?" Catherine asked. "I need to go, PC... whoever, please keep this woman away from me."

Cronk smiled at her. "I would like to check your..." He looked at Lola.

"Right jacket pocket," she said for she had looked back on the video and seen her put the bottle there.

"What?!" Catherine asked. "You have no right, do you have a warrant?"

"No, but I have probable cause," he said.

"What is that?" Catherine asked as she tried to back away but was bumped by a group of people and almost pushed into the PC.

"It is reasonable grounds to believe that a particular person has committed a crime, especially to justify making a search or preferring a charge."

Lola chuckled, but kept it so he couldn't see. Catherine was not asking for the definition, but for what had given him probable cause. Smiling at Catherine, who smiled in return, possibly thinking that Lola was agreeing with her that the PC didn't have it. Lola was hating the thought of, well, not really, bursting her bubble, Lola showed her the video of her putting the bottle in her pocket.

Catherine crumpled to the floor, ably caught by Cronk. He helped her up and took her over to a seat. Once she was sitting down he pulled latex gloves from his pocket and checked her jacket, pulling out a bottle that matched the ones in Maria's kit.

"How did that get there?" Catherine asked.

Cronk chuckled as he put the bottle into an evidence bag. "Don't worry, we have video evidence of how it got there."

CONVINCING THE BOSS

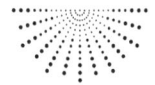

*A*ll the friends were standing around Catherine. Alice was mad, her back was to them and her arms were folded. Lola had asked her not to say anything to Catherine until DI Turner arrived. However, she was finding it hard to keep quiet.

Sassy tapped against her leg and Alice looked down, her whole demeanor changed and she scooped the Frenchie into her arms and cuddle her close. "I knew you would help, you are so clever."

"And hungry," Sassy said.

Lola chuckled just as the DI arrived in front of them. His face was stern and his eyes drawn; he turned a menacing gaze onto the young PC.

"Well, Cronk, explain yourself," DI Turner said.

PC Cronk looked a little worried but Lola flashed him a smile. It seemed to help and he handed over Lola's phone. So far the video was still on there, they would forward it, but wanted the DI to see it first. She didn't know for sure but felt this would be more convincing that it wasn't altered in any way.

"What is this?" Turner asked.

Cronk showed him the evidence bag containing the bottle.

"Who?" Turner asked.

They stepped back to reveal Catherine, her hands in handcuffs, sitting on a bench looking most dejected.

"Well, I never expected that," Turner said. He turned his fierce gaze on Catherine and she wilted a little more. "What do you have to say for yourself?" he said.

"I... this is all a setup. I lost my ring and I found that bottle." Catherine was looking a little more confident, it was clear that she had an idea that she thought might save her. "I recognized it as Maria's and was going to bring it to the police as evidence." Her head was held a little higher and there was a smug expression on her face.

"Never lost ring," Sassy said.

"Shush." Lola stroked her back.

"She telling porkies."

"I know, don't worry." Lola felt color touch her cheeks, she had just spoken to the dog in front of all these people, what would they think?

"You are so funny," Alice said and put Sassy down. "And, you are very heavy."

"Not fat, not had enough donuts!" Sassy was looking up with expectation lighting her eyes. "Could eat more."

Lola dropped another treat and tried to bring her mind back to the matter at hand, they needed Catherine to confess.

It looked like Alice was already on it, for she approached her friend. "Why did you kill her?"

"Oh, I never meant to kill her," Catherine said. "Just to make her poorly." Catherine's eyes closed and she dropped her head, hair covering her face.

This had been one of the clues that Lola had followed, Catherine had been shocked at Una's death and also confused about the timing. Lola searched her memory until she could recall what she had said.

"I don't know how this happened, how can she be dead? Why did it happen after judging, it makes no sense that she's dead. I just... I just don't believe it."

It had been a strange thing to say and had tinkled on Lola's spidey sense even back then. However, she had pushed it aside as she wanted the killer to be someone else.

"Why!" Alice almost screamed.

Catherine looked thoroughly miserable. "It was all a terrible mistake. I believed that Raoul and Felix were making it a condition of Una's judging appointment that Queenie was taken from me. Oh, what a fool I have been."

Alice put a gentle hand on her shoulder. "Go on."

"I believed that if we didn't win, or the show was canceled then it would all go away. I was so afraid that I was going to be used as a drug mule or something worse."

"Why do people always think that?" Raoul asked. "We just wanted Queenie to come home for a visit."

"But you would never have won," Alice said. "I don't understand why you did... why you killed her!"

"I think I understand," Lola said. "Una was feeling the effects of the poison. I don't believe she was well enough to tell us who the killer was, but she knew. Her only course of action was to crown them the winner and hope that would bring its own suspicion. It did."

"I swear, I didn't mean to kill her. I was just so afraid."

"We have enough," Turner said and hesitated for a moment before turning to PC Cronk. "Well done, do you have any more evidence?"

Lola nodded at him, they had discussed this earlier.

Cronk leaned over Catherine and pulled the slide from her hair. "I think this will match the one in Una's room. It proves Catherine was in there this morning."

"Oh, I wondered where I'd lost that and I only brought one pair with me."

"Take her away," Turner said.

Cronk had a big smile on his face as Catherine was led away and soon the friends were alone.

"What happens to all the dogs?" Alice asked. "Queenie and Willow?"

"I would like to keep Willow," Gunter said. "Una had no relations that she would let her go to. I will love and care for her and maybe, use Una's journal to continue her work."

"That sounds wonderful," Alice said. "I know she would have liked that. We must become friends too, you are always welcome to come and see me."

Gunter's eyes widened a little but then his face softened. "I would like that. I must go, the dogs have had a hard day." Gunter turned and walked away.

"What about Queenie?" Alice asked. "I feel so sorry for her, Catherine had no family that are doggy people. I know that none of them will want her. What is to become of her?

"I have a few calls to make. Let's meet up at the Cottage Tea Room for tea and a bite to eat," Lola said.

"The tea room with proper cups?" Tilly asked. "Now I've found it, I'd rather not go anywhere else.

"Of course."

"May we come?" Raoul asked. "It may be distasteful but we would still like Queenie. We would care for her well. I realize there will be many people who want her and we have no right but maybe we can arrange with new people for a visit?"

"Go join the others and give me a few minutes," Lola said, "and thank you for your help. I'm sorry I misjudged you. You are good men and you helped bring a killer to justice.

Raoul and Felix stood tall, their chests puffed out with pride.

WHAT ABOUT QUEENIE?

*L*ola took Sassy outside for a visit.

"I did good, did I?" Sassy asked after a few minutes of sniffies and finding the right spot.

"You certainly did." Lola was feeling very proud of her little dog. It must have been so hard for Sassy to keep still and quiet to get the evidence but she had done so admirably.

"I could sniffies night night as soon as I got in the shiny room. I wanted to tell you but remembered to be quiet. It was hard, made me hungry." Her mouth was open, her tongue lolling out and there was a big smile on her face.

"I'm sure that Alice and Tilly will have a treat for you."

"They are the bestest," Sassy said and turned to trot back to the hall.

Lola cleared her throat.

Sassy turned and looked at her and then dropped onto the floor and rolled on her back. "Sorry, you the bestest too."

"Let me just make these calls, before we go back in," Lola said and they wandered over to a bench. Sassy found the sniffies from the trash can very intriguing and Lola left her to it while she dialed Patricia.

"Lola," Patricia said. "How is it all going, can I do anything else for you?"

"We have the killer, thanks in part to you. It was Catherine Guzman, a friend of the victim's, unfortunately."

"Oh, I'm sorry, but I'm pleased I could help. Is there something else?"

"Alice tells me that you are very involved with a few dog breeders and that you would understand the ownership of a dog. Well, what happens to a dog under these circumstances? When the owner is going to jail?"

"Of course, if there are no relatives to take the dog then it would be back to the original contract of sale. Not everyone has conditions in their contract when they sell puppies, not everyone has a contract, but the good breeders all do, and they are pretty standard," Patricia explained the most likely scenario to Lola.

"That is really helpful, thanks."

Lola dialed again.

"Lola, it is great to hear your voice," Linc said. "I'm feeling very important with two calls in a day. I can't wait for a week on Friday, to see you again."

Lola could almost see the twinkle in his blue eyes and feared she may be being teased, a little. It felt nice, like a start. "We caught the killer," Lola said. "I wanted you to know."

"That's great, you and the gang are amazing. Who was it?"

Lola didn't like to tell him that it had been Sassy who had sealed the deal, maybe she could in the future. She missed not having anyone know that she could hear her dog. "It was the friend, Catherine."

"Oh, wow. I didn't see that coming."

"How is the ghost research coming on?"

A chuckle came down the phone. "There are a lot of people who believe, but none of it has helped me. I can tell you are in a rush, why don't we talk about this when we meet up?"

"That would be great. How about we do it sooner. Could you make Wednesday for a coffee at the Lakeside Garden Center?"

"Brilliant... how about I pick you up at 12 and we have lunch?"

Lola felt her heart stop for a moment, she wanted to say yes and, at that moment, she felt a tap on her leg. "Can Sassy come?" Oh, no, had she just asked that? She sounded like a teenager.

"Of course, I will see you then."

Lola knew what this meant and after she had hung up, she did a quick search on the internet, Facebook, and for reviews on the Henvel kennels and on how they kept their dogs. There was nothing but praise for the two men and for the dogs they had bred and sent on to new homes. Many people still kept in touch with the men and they had a page on their website with dogs from their kennel. The pride they had in them was clear in the photos and there were too many testimonials, all written differently, all saying different things but all praising the men and how they looked after the dogs.

This put Lola's mind at ease, there was the right thing to do and the legally correct thing to do, it looked like this time, the two were aligned.

"Shall we go see Tilly and Alice?" Lola asked.

Sassy was immediately in front of her staring up with eager and hungry eyes.

Lola found her friends at the Cottage Tea Room, they were looking very glum and Sassy rushed straight to Alice.

"What is it?" Lola asked. Alice, Tilly, Raoul, and Felix all looked terribly despondent. Though she understood the shock of the murder and finding out that Catherine was the killer, even so, Lola had hoped that they would start to feel better.

That was when she noticed that Queenie was not there. "Where is she?" Lola asked.

"It was Turner, he had PC Cronk take her away. It seems she will go to the kennels." Alice was cuddling Sassy to her but the misery on her face was clear.

Lola took a seat and Tilly offered her a coffee and a cake from the stand. Lola took the coffee but shook her head at the cake. Sassy gave her some serious side eye but she ignored it. "Do not worry, I think I have a way out of this."

"Really?" Alice asked, feeding Sassy a little bit of Victoria sponge cake.

"Yes." Lola turned to Raoul and Felix. "When you sell your puppies do you have any sort of contract?"

Raoul's face broke into a grin and he turned to Felix and hugged him. "Of course, of course, we do. This is marvelous."

"I don't understand," Alice said.

"I think I do." Tilly was also smiling. "You tell her." She nodded at Raoul who was finding it hard to keep his smile in control.

"It is standard amongst most contracts for puppies. If the owner no longer wants the puppy or something happens to them, then the breeder has the right to have the dog back."

"Then, she is yours?" Alice asked as a smile broke out on her face.

"We believe so," Felix said as he tapped away on his phone. "I will send for a copy of the contract, now how do we get her back?"

Lola chuckled. "I have PC Cronk's phone number. She dialed it quickly and told the PC the good news.

It was just a matter of minutes before he appeared with Queenie. Lola was pleased to see that the dog ran to Raoul and Felix and seemed completely at home with them. Though she would no doubt miss Catherine terribly, she would have a good home with people who loved her and would spoil her as she deserved.

Raoul was now on the floor with his arm around the dog, Queenie was licking his ears, her tail wagging so fast it was almost a blur.

LUNCH DATE

It was Wednesday, just before lunch and Lola stood in the office of her new home. She was almost ready to move in but hadn't made the decision yet. Living with Tanya and her boyfriend, Detective Sergeant Wayne Foster was both enjoyable and useful.

Wayne had helped her on past cases, and even though she wanted her own freedom and wanted to give the couple their space, she was loath to move out. It was strange. When she first saw the old garage it was perfect. An office downstairs where she could meet clients, keep files, and do the admin work for her private investigator business. On the wall behind the reception hung a fabulous painting of the view from her window. In the sky was the Red Arrow's aerobatics team and down on the ground was Sassy watching them fly over. It was signed by her good friend Louisa Meek, once a disgruntled PA, now a famous artist.

Upstairs was a lovely apartment, or flat as Alice had described it. Outside, there was plenty of parking for customers, not that she expected that many. And a nice-sized garden for Sassy.

The front of the property had needed to be redone as well as the renovations inside. These were complete and all that remained was for Lola to move in.

She looked out at the resin driveway in front of her and remembered a time when there was a hole in the tarmac and a plethora of policemen around it. When she first came to see the property, her little bulldog had been interested in the area. Seeing strange men dig it up soon after, it didn't take long for Sassy to work out that there was a buried body there.

Lola shuddered. That case was long behind them now, but it reminded her why she loved doing this. She had brought justice to a young woman who would not have received it without her. At the moment, she had five cases on her books. None were very interesting. They were three divorces, one background check, and one where she was tracking down a lost relative following a death. None of these were urgent and in some ways, she wondered why she did them.

With the trust fund left to her by her parents and the money left by a Russian, for helping solve his son's murder, she had no need to work. Then her eyes fell on a corkboard on the reception wall. It was covered with letters and cards of thanks.

These cases may not be the most exciting, but they meant a lot to her clients. There was a big bunch of flowers on the coffee table in the reception area. They had arrived this morning from Gunter. He was back home with Winnie and had sent her some photos which she planned to share with Alice.

Gunter was free because of her and Winnie looked very happy.

Raoul and Felix had also sent a gift, theirs had been chocolates for her and dog chocolates for Sassy. The little Frenchie was so pleased to be remembered and knew exactly where her treats were stored, though Lola was rationing them.

"Linc here soon," Sassy said.

Lola checked her watch. "No, it will be about 15 minutes."

"No, here now." Sassy ran to the window and looked out as a deep red Landrover Defender pulled onto the driveway.

Lola chuckled. "How did you know?"

Sassy turned and gave her a strange look. "Just know... you not know?"

When Linc came in he looked a tad stressed. His tawny brown hair was a little rumpled and there were deep smudges beneath his blue eyes.

"Are you okay?" she asked.

Linc's eyes opened wide along with his mouth. "It's nice to see you too."

Lola chuckled and could see that Sassy was sitting before him with her cutest expression.

Linc bent down and rubbed her head. "At least you know how to greet me. I'm so pleased to see you."

"Pleased to see you too, any treats?" Sassy asked with the cutest grumble and groan.

As if by magic, Linc pulled a little bit of cheese treat out of his pocket. "Let's keep this between us two." He winked and Lola couldn't help but smile.

"Okay," Sassy said. "I keep lots of secrets." She was trying to keep her barking quiet, but in her excitement, it was easy for Lola to understand it.

"Now, shall we?" Linc stood up and held out his arm and bowed slightly, like an old-fashioned English gentleman.

"It would be my pleasure." Lola took his arm and tried to fight down her panic. This was fine, it was just a meal, and no one was going to die.

* * *

Lola, Linc, and Sassy were sitting at a table looking over the lake at the Lakeside Garden Center. They had eaten a nice lunch, both going for the lasagna and chips, as fries were called. Lola was trying to get used to the language, but some of it was strange.

"That was very nice," Lola said as she sipped on her Latte.

"Yeah, I enjoyed it."

For once it was not Lola who was stilted with the conversation. Though she was always fine talking to people in normal situations, when dating was involved, she tended to clam up. Today, however, it was Linc who was quiet and he, frankly, looked terrible.

At first, she had taken it a little personally. Maybe, he was no longer interested in her. She would not be surprised, for she had been a little uncommunicative. Now, though, she had a different idea. He had something on his mind and the investigator in her wanted to know what it was.

"What is the problem?" Lola asked as she noted that Sassy was trying to peer around the corner and was looking at a bush planted there. It was one of these fur bushes, that only grew so tall. They could be kept in pots and were all-year-round color. What was up with her? Was it a cat? They wandered around the café area, but Sassy had never bothered about them before. Or maybe it was a chicken, they too were often looking for scraps of food from the tables. Then there were the ducks, geese, swans, or the two black swans on the lake. However, Sassy appeared to be looking higher up than could account for any of this.

Linc was talking and Lola realized she had missed the first few words, so she pulled her mind back to the table.

"... my friend, he fears that he is being haunted. I have tried to quash the idea but it is making him... paranoid and I don't know what to do."

"Tell me what he is seeing... or why he thinks such things."

Linc let out a breath. "It's such a relief to talk to someone who can understand and listen."

Sassy was leaning so far over that she was almost slipping off Lola's knee. She wanted to ask the dog what it was but Linc was still talking.

"He says doors keep opening, things move in the house and he sees shadows. Even his food has gone missing at times."

"That is very strange," Lola said. "The doors and things moving could be a draught... I don't suppose it could be..." Lola shuddered she could cope with most things but... "rats?"

"No, I checked for that. I have to tell you that Jimmy had it bad. He lost a lot of friends in Afghanistan. Maybe, he is just seeing things. The house was his father's... and I don't think they were on good terms. I'm sure you know how it can be." Linc ran a hand through his hair and it stuck on end even more.

Lola did and the words brought back her own rush of guilt. If only she had seen her parents one more time.

"I do think he could just be drunk, though. He has been known to partake and he could be eating the food himself."

Lola wanted to chuckle, this was a good man and he was losing sleep over it. "I'm sure there is a valid explanation, why don't we investigate it for him?"

"That would be wonderful." Linc let out a breath and relaxed. "What is she looking at?" he asked noticing Sassy.

"Tilly and Alice are hiding and giggling behind that bush," Sassy said. "It silly, but fun."

Lola peered even closer at the bush in question and she could see a flash of bright yellow, the sort of fluorescent yellow that only Alice would wear.

"I think we're being watched," Lola said.

Linc's eyebrows raised. "Is it trouble?" There was now an alertness about him, the fatigue had gone.

"Easy soldier," Lola said. "This is embarrassing, but I think it is my friends, Tilly and Alice."

Linc let out a peal of laughter. "They have both contacted me to make sure that today was still on. I guess they really care about you."

Lola grinned. "Wait here," she said to Sassy. The Frenchie grumbled as Lola got up and put her in the chair, Linc did a mock salute.

Quickly, Lola made her way across the paved area and into the café. The café was between them and where her friends were hiding. She walked through it coming out of the other entrance. She skirted around the side until she was behind Tilly and Alice.

It was quite a sight, Tilly had on a brown tweed skirt suit and next to her, both of them bending over to peer through the bush, was Alice in a bright yellow and green shell suit.

Lola cleared her throat and the two ladies jumped up and turned around.

"Oh," Tilly said.

"Ah," Alice said.

"Guess we've been caught." Tilly chuckled. "We just came in case you needed any backup, but we will go, as it seems like you're having a great time."

"Not so fast," Lola said and put a stern expression on her face.

The two ladies paled.

"Come and join us," Lola added.

"Oh, we shouldn't," Alice said trying to skirt around her.

"No, we don't want to gooseberry," Tilly added.

"Don't worry, we are not going to be necking at the table, come on."

Lola walked them back to the table, and just as they got there a woman came over with tears in her eyes.

"Alice, oh, I'm so glad to see you. I was just meeting Rowena here and then we were on our way to see you." The woman was short and thin wearing black trousers and a black blouse. Her short black hair was peppered with gray. The woman beside her had longer blonde hair that was in a bun on her head. She was of a similar build and also all in black.

Something about that made Lola's heart kick up a beat.

As the three women stepped away from the table, Linc ordered more tea and Lola wondered, *what now?*

OH OH

"Oh, oh," Sassy said as Alice left the table.

"What is it, Sweetie?" Lola asked.

Linc raised an eyebrow and then smiled. Lola would have to be careful; if she wanted to get to know this man, the last thing she needed was for him to think she was a dotty old lady.

For a moment, Sassy's ears pricked up at the word sweetie, but then it dawned on her that this was another name that Lola used. "Both ladies really upset and sad, I think Alice has more bad news coming."

"I wonder what that is all about?" Tilly asked.

"I'm more interested in seeing you both here," Linc said with his right eyebrow raised. "Isn't that a coincidence!"

Tilly's mouth opened and she blushed a pretty pink color beneath her gray hair and round glasses. Pushing them back up her nose, she screwed up her eyes and wrinkled her nose. It was clear that she was thinking. "Oh, I may as well admit it, we were watching you."

"I didn't realize I was so interesting," Linc said, puffing out his chest. He winked at Lola. "It looks like you might have competition."

"No, no," Tilly swatted at his arm, a look of sheer horror on her face until she realized that he was teasing. "Oh, you."

"It is lovely to see you both again," Linc said and waved at a waitress. "Can we have more cake and tea please?"

The girl took the order and left.

Shortly after, Alice came back, her face was white and her friends had gone.

"What is it?" Tilly asked as Alice slumped into a chair. Before she could pull her chair forward, Sassy had commando crawled from Lola's knee and across the gap onto Alice's knee.

"Oh, look at you, cheering me up." Alice wiped at her eyes which were shining with unshed tears.

"That was a very good friend of mine, Claire Hickinbottom, with her friend, Rowena Webb. It appears that Rowena's husband has gone missing and the police think she killed him.

Sassy lay on Alice's lap and covered her eyes with her paws.

"Are they going to arrest her?" Lola asked.

"They don't have enough evidence yet. There is no body, just a witness that says they saw something, and Theodore is missing. Claire is worried out of her mind… she has lost her husband and now the police are harassing her." Alice said. "Rowena wanted to meet Claire here to tell her all about it and then they were going to come and see me. I told them about you and gave Claire your details."

"Maybe I should go and talk to her." Lola was itching to get on the case.

"I'm sorry, but Claire does not believe it is necessary yet." Alice shrugged.

"Tea and cake," Linc said trying to distract Alice.

"Oh, you are so kind," she said and took a bit of cake, breaking off the first bit and feeding it to Sassy.

"Nice, toffee!" Sassy said.

"What did the witness see?" Lola asked.

Alice chewed for a moment and then took a sip of tea. "They said they were walking past and heard screaming. A woman screaming at a man. They stopped and saw the woman hit the man with a champagne bottle. Apparently, the cork popped and the man fell to the floor. The woman then continued to hit him again and again. The woman fled and rushed to a phone box to call the police.

"No cell?" Lola said.

Alice looked confused.

"Mobile," Tilly said.

"Oh, no, I didn't ask. What do you think we should do?" Alice looked so miserable, that for the moment, Sassy had forgotten cake and was leaning against her, offering what comfort she could.

"I could go talk to her," Lola said.

"I don't think you should," Alice shrugged. "At the moment, she is convinced that this is all some joke and that her husband will be back soon."

"Okay, I will leave it," Lola said. "But you have to let me get involved as soon as possible. The quicker the better as clues can dissipate."

"Sniffies stay long time, surely, you can sniffy that!" Sassy said.

"How long?" Lola asked looking down at Sassy, as she looked up she realized that all eyes were on her. "Sorry, thinking aloud." She shrugged.

"I think I should take you home," Tilly said.

"Yes, it has been a trying time recently." Alice turned to Lola. "I will go see Claire in a couple of days. I will get you involved if this is more than just a prank."

Lola squeezed Tilly's hand and bid them both goodbye. Once they were gone Linc turned to her.

"So, are you going to leave it?" There was a slight knowing smile on his face.

"I might just make a few inquiries." Lola returned the smile. "My friend, Wayne Foster will know something."

"I expected nothing else. And if I ever pop my cork in unexpected ways, it's you I'd want to investigate. Now, let's go take this little rascal for a walk around the nature reserve."

Sassy was instantly sitting in front of him.

Though Lola was itching to get on the case, she knew there was nothing she could do just yet. Later, she would talk to Wayne, but for now, this seemed like a good distraction. Maybe she could even grow to like having company.

Read on for 1 Frenchie (can be enjoyed by other dogs but has been approved by a very hungry Frenchie) and 1 Human recipe...

The next book Popped his Cork will be out soon, to find out when join my newsletter and receive 3 FREE stories and more to come.

You can now grab the first 6 Bulldog on the Case books in one great value box set and also FREE with Kindle Unlimited

ICED CHERRY BAKEWELL TRAY BAKE RECIPE

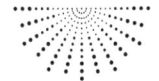

Ingredients:

You can use prebought sweet pastry or make your own.

For the Pastry:

115 g or 1/2 cup unsalted butter

220 g or 1 3/4 cups plain flour

100 g or 1/2 cup caster sugar

1 large egg

For the Filling:

6 tbs seedless strawberry jam/jelly

200 g or 1 3/4 sticks softened unsalted butter

200g or 1 cup caster sugar

4 medium eggs

125g or 1 cup self-raising flour

120 g or 1 cup of ground almonds

2 tsp of almond extract

For the Icing:

312 g or 2 1/2 cups icing sugar

3 tbs water

16 Glacé cherries

. . .

Directions:

For the Pastry:

Using a mixer, mix together the softened butter and flour until it is the consistency of fine crumb.

Add the sugar and combine.

Add the egg and mix until a dough starts to form.

On a lightly floured surface, knead the dough until it is smooth and even.

Form into a ball and flatten slightly, put aside in cling-film, and place in the fridge to rest for approx. 30 minutes.

For the Filling:

. . .

Preheat the oven to 200C/400F.

On a lightly floured surface, roll out the pastry to fit the base and sides of a greased 13 x 9-inch baking tray.

Spread the jam over the pastry base.

Using a mixer, beat the softened butter and sugar until smooth and creamy

Beat in the eggs, one at a time.

Add 1 tbs of ground almonds after each egg.

Add the flour, the remaining almonds, and the almond extract, and stir well.

Pour the mixture over the jam, spreading it out to make an even layer.

Bake for 30 - 35 minutes until well risen, firm and golden.

Remove from the oven and leave to cool in the pan.

For the Icing:

Mix together the icing sugar and 3 tbs of water to make a nice thick icing.

When the tart is cool, pour the icing on top, spreading out evenly.

Decorate with glacé cherries, and leave to set.

Cut the tart into squares, serve, and enjoy.

Can be frozen for up to 3 months or kept in the fridge for a few days.

SASSY APPROVED EASY FISH DOG TREATS

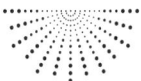

Ingredients:

- 1 cup of pumpkin
- 2 cups of salmon
- 2 cups of white fish
- 2 cups of fish stock
- 2 1/2 cups of rice or oat flour
- 3 tbsp psyllium husk
- 2 tbsp seaweed granules
- 2 eggs

Directions:

1. In a pan of hot water, cook all the fish, using a medium heat. Taking around 15 to 20 minutes.

2. Once the fish is cooked, remove from the heat and leave to coo.
3. Preheat the oven to 350F (180C).
4. In a bowl, add the pumpkin, fish, and fish stock and blend until a nice, smooth fishy paste. If it's a bit too stiff and dry, add more fish stock, a tablespoon at a time. If it's a little too wet that is fine - you can always add more flour later on.
5. Set aside the rest of the fish stock in case you need it later.
6. Add the dry ingredients to a large bowl and mix thoroughly.
7. Next, pour the fishy paste into the dry ingredients.
8. Add the eggs and beat the whole thing together.
9. If this is hard to mix and too dry, add a little more fish water stock a tablespoon at a time.
10. If it's a little too wet, add more flour.
11. You are looking for a very thick, grainy batter consistency. It should be stiff but spreadable.
12. If you have them use silicone molds to suit the dogs size or put a blob on a silicone baking sheet on a baking tray.
13. Use a little fat or soft butter to grease the molds or sheet.

14. Fill the molds or put on baking tray.
15. Bake for approximately 10 minutes depending on the size of your molds, treats. They should be a golden orange-yellow color and will be lightly crisped on the outside.
16. They may be a little soft when cooked, but that's fine. You can use like this, but they will keep better and be crispier, if you dehydrate for 3 hours or as needed.

ALSO BY ROSIE SAMS

Grab free short stories and be the first to find out when Rosie has a new release by joining her free newsletter

* * *

You can now grab the first 6 Bulldog on the Case books in one great value box set and also FREE with Kindle Unlimited

Follow Rosie on BookBub – go here and click the red follow button

Follow Rosie on Amazon – go here click the yellow follow button

If you enjoyed this book, Rosie and Lila would appreciate it if you left a review on Amazon or Goodreads.

©Copyright 2022 Rosie Sams
All Rights Reserved
Rosie Sams

License Notes
This Book is licensed for personal enjoyment only. It may not be resold. Your continued respect for author's rights is appreciated.

This story is a work of fiction; any resemblance to people is purely coincidence. All places, names, events, businesses, etc. are used in a fictional manner. All characters are from the imagination of the author.

Printed in Great Britain
by Amazon